SLOW DOWN,

SO I CAN TELL YOU I LOVE YOU

SLOW DOWN,

SO I CAN TELL YOU I LOVE YOU

TAMMY YOUNG

CITADEL PRESS
Kensington Publishing Corp.
www.kensingtonbooks.com

CITADEL PRESS books are published by

Kensington Publishing Corp.
850 Third Avenue
New York, NY 10022

All Kensington titles, imprints, and distrbuted lines are available at special quantity discounts for bulk purchases for sales promotions, premiums, fund raising, educational, or institutional use. Special book excerpts or customized printings can also be created to fit specific needs. For details, write or phone the office of the Kensington special sales manager: Kensington Publishing Corp., 850 Third Avenue, New York, NY 10022, attn: Special Sales Department, phone 1-800-221-2647.

First Citadel printing October 2001

10 9 8 7 6 5 4 3 2 1

Printed in the United States of America

Library of Congress Control Number 2001091873

ISBN 0-8065-2208-9

To Nickolas, Heather, and Brandi, who teach me more each day about what it means to be a mother. Their innocence and their wisdom inspire me to be the very best I can be for them.

The man may teach by doing, and not otherwise. If he can communicate himself he can teach, but not with words. He teaches who gives, and he learns who receives. There is no teaching until the pupil is brought into the same state or principle in which you are; a transfusion takes place; he is you and you are he; then is a teaching, and by no unfriendly chance or bad company can he ever quite lose the benefit.

–Emerson, *Spiritual Laws*

Table of Contents

Foreword

I n my career as a clinical psychologist, I have had the opportunity to work with many children and adolescents with AD/HD and their families. I have also been fortunate in my workshops to talk with many parents of youngsters with AD/HD as well as the teachers and other professionals who are involved with these children. These interactions have been invaluable in helping me to appreciate the special struggles, frustrations, questions, and joys associated with parenting a child with AD/HD. I have witnessed firsthand the emotional and physical stress that many of these parents experience as they attempt to raise children who are impulsive and unpredictable, who act before they think, and who often live in the moment so that their behavior does not benefit from previous learning or a consideration of possible consequences.

I discovered in my conversations with these youth that many are burdened by feelings of low self-esteem and inadequacy, of not fitting in with their peers, of anxiety and anger, and of a belief that their situation would not improve. In essence, many of these children had lost one of the most important commodities we possess as people, namely, hope. A loss of hope often triggers self-defeating ways of coping reflected in such behaviors as quitting, blaming others, drug use, anger, and even suicide. It is not unusual to find that the frustration and despair felt by these children also exist in their parents, parents who constantly question their own competencies and struggle with anxiety, sorrow, confusion, and fear of what the future holds for their child.

As I reflect upon my work with children with AD/HD, I realize that initially much of my focus was on the negative, spotlighting the problems and shortcomings of these children, struggling with my own feelings of pessimism about the direction their lives would take, and even being somewhat accusatory or judgmental as I implored them to "try harder" or "put in more of an effort." But slowly, as I gained experience with youngsters with AD/HD and their parents, this pathological perspective was replaced by a more positive mind-set or approach. I came to marvel at the courage, determination, hope, and perseverance demonstrated by these families even when faced with great adversity. I found myself using the word "resilient" with increasing frequency, wondering why some children with AD/HD find success and contentment in their adult lives, while others remain trapped by feelings of low self-esteem, anger, and hopelessness.

In my journey from pathology and pessimism to hope and resilience, I reviewed the burgeoning research about resilience and spoke with many resilient individuals. I attempted to understand the mind-set of resilient children so that I might build guideposts for my interventions. But in my quest to understand the mind-set of resilient children, I quickly recognized that I must also examine the mind-set of parents and other caregivers who appear to be more successful in nurturing hope and resilience in their children. In what ways do these adults view their children and themselves that help to guide them down a path of resilience? I wondered why some parents were successful in using a wide range of strategies, while other parents using similar strategies reported continued frustration and failure. Certainly the behaviors of some youngsters with AD/HD were more problematic than other children with the same diagnosis, but I also came to believe that the success of any intervention was based, in great part, on the mindset of the adult using the intervention.

This last statement should not be interpreted as judgmental. I refrain from using labels such as "bad" or "good" parents. Rather, I believe we must strive to free ourselves from a judgmental or accusatory stance. Instead, we must adopt a perspective housed in understanding and compassion, a perspective from which we can more effectively articulate those factors that provide us with the knowledge and strength to parent or teach children with AD/HD in ways that will maximize their opportunities for success.

In the past decade, we have witnessed the publication of several excellent books related to parenting a child with AD/HD. Some are written by professionals in the field, others by parents, and still others by individuals who wear both hats, namely, professionals who have a child with AD/HD. Tammy Young, a special education teacher, a counselor, and the mother of two children with AD/HD, has written a truly remarkable book that deserves its place among the best in the field. *Slow Down, So I Can Tell You I Love You* is not only filled with a wealth of specific information pertaining to all aspects of raising a child with AD/HD, but it also eloquently attends to the belief system held by the parent. Tammy courageously shares her journey, her self-examination, her struggles, her pain, her triumphs, and her joys. She describes what she learned in her training as a spiritual counselor and the ways in which spirituality changed how she viewed the role of a parent and the development of a child. Tammy's shift from a perspective that focused on pathology and deficits to one that focused on the beauty and strengths of each child is captured in her statement:

> It was [a] journey of discovery that eventually led me to realize that there was much more to the issue of AD/HD than I could possibly have known. The whole approach I had espoused . . . was rooted in the belief that there was something wrong with these children. I had been talking about how to change them. I had approached the entire situation as if these children were wild horses to be broken when, in fact, they were here, in perfect form, with their own lessons to learn. Their presence provided me with an opportunity for inner growth. I saw for the first time that it was I who must change.

Tammy challenges us to examine the ways in which we accept our children with AD/HD. She looks at parenting a child with AD/HD through a lens of acceptance, an appreciation of each child's unique temperament and learning style, and a deep-rooted belief that children are our gifts. All features of parenting are guided by this mind-set, by what Tammy calls "spiritual parenting." In hearing the words "spiritual parenting," some might immediately, but wrongfully, believe that it is a form of parenting predicated on "letting kids do whatever they want," not considering medication as an important treatment intervention, and not holding children accountable for their actions. Tammy shows us that accepting and unconditionally loving our children with AD/HD is an integral part of an approach that teaches children they are responsible for their actions, that a diagnosis of AD/HD must never be used as an excuse for unacceptable behaviors, and that they can take increasing control of their lives.

As I read this impressive book, I realized that one need not be very religious or a member of a specific religion to embrace the philosophy captured on each page. Tammy presents a blueprint for parenting that is applicable to all children and predicated on such humanistic principles as empathy, respect, dignity, responsibility, and self-discipline. If this book only contained a description of spiritual parenting, it would still be very commendable, encouraging all of us to examine our own attitudes toward our children. However, what adds to the power of the book is the wide spectrum of information it covers about AD/HD including the components of the diagnostic phase, the issues of medication, the importance of parents working closely together, the challenges of the single-parent home, discipline, teaching responsibility, characteristics of the oppositional defiant child, strategies for working closely with the child's school to ensure an optimal school environment, and special education and other laws and services that apply to youngsters with AD/HD.

Near the end of her book, Tammy writes:

> There is a reason that your AD/HD child is with you. You and your child are on a beautiful journey together. It does not have to be riddled with pain and crisis; it can, instead, be a fabulous journey of love and enlightenment. You can experience in yourself, and with your child, the joy of becoming.

This sentiment should not be seen as flowery language without substance. Having read this book, I have no hesitation in saying that it is filled with substance, that it provides us with important information, and it provokes us in an empathic way to reflect upon the principles of our parenting. I believe that this book will be read and reread, not only by parents, but by teachers and other professionals who work with children with AD/HD and their families. Each time it is read, new insights will be achieved about children with AD/HD, but perhaps even more important, each reading will help us to develop new insights about ourselves and our own journey. Tammy's book represents a gift to all of us.

–Robert B. Brooks, Ph.D.,
Faculty, Harvard Medical School

Preface

In 1993, two of my children were diagnosed with Attention Deficit/Hyperactivity Disorder. That diagnosis sent our family spinning into a world we knew little about. I began to devour information about AD/HD, everything from the characteristics of it to the practical applications in my life. I became the parent of two AD/HD children; AD/HD became the prevalent issue in my life.

My world was consumed with medical appointments, monitoring a variety of medications in various combinations and dosages, and behavior management programs. Nothing seemed to make a lasting difference. I was overwhelmed and depleted. I felt that I was a failure as a parent. Learning that other parents of AD/HD children were experiencing the same difficulties as my family provided a degree of comfort and hope. My family was not alone.

By 1994, I was involved in the start-up of a chapter of Children and Adults with Attention Deficit Disorder, CHADD, in Albuquerque. That same year, I graduated from the University of New Mexico with a degree in Special Education and immediately began teaching in public schools. As I worked with students with AD/HD in the classroom, my commitment to this exceptional group of children grew. I was able to see the impact of AD/HD both as a parent and as a teacher. With this dual perspective, I began to see a path for change for our children. Through the workshops I facilitated as an officer of CHADD, I encouraged teachers and parents to have realistic expectations. Each time I spoke, the feedback I received was surprising. The evaluations came back overwhelmingly positive. I felt I could definitely make a difference.

In the summer of 1994, I was involved in a serious auto accident resulting in a head injury. Many of the issues I received therapy for, as a result of this injury, were the same issues my children struggle with because of AD/HD. I gained a great deal of insight about what my children go through because of this injury and the subsequent treatments.

Every big event in life brings with it an inner transformation. The most profound effect that I experienced was a spiritual transformation. I became aware that there was a part of me that was completely untouched by my injury. As the injury healed, old wounds healed as well. I began a journey of spiritual transformation that was often painful, but richly rewarding. Ultimately, this spiritual inquiry led me to complete the Religious Science Professional Practitioner Studies Program for licensure as a spiritual counselor.

It was this journey of discovery that eventually led me to realize that there was much more to the issue of AD/HD than I could possibly have known. The whole approach I had espoused until that time was rooted in the belief that there was something wrong with these children. I had been talking about how to change them. I had approached the entire situation as if these children were wild horses to be broken when, in fact, they were here, in perfect form, with their own lessons to learn. Their presence provided me with an opportunity for inner growth. I saw for the first time that it was I who must change.

Many of the strategies I had advocated up to this point are still strategies I recommend today in my work as an educational consultant and child advocate. Much of the information I present to teachers and parents has not changed. What has been completely transformed is my view of these children and my devotion to honoring the spirit of each child, to honor and care for and teach these children with love and appreciation. I see the precious innocence inherent in every child present in every moment. My message is not about changing them but about nurturing their unique gifts and talents. They have a great deal to learn, as do we all. A wonderful opportunity is presented to each one of us to grow and learn together with our children.

As a parent, I have much to share that illustrates how these children can liven up the life of a family as well as the grief and difficulties associated with the job of raising a child with AD/HD. A larger story that weaves through the fabric of this book is of the great love that has evolved between myself and my children. This includes an element of understanding and compassion that I find to be rare and beautiful; I know my children. Because I accept them for who they are and care about the root of their feelings and actions and because I love them for who they are and not who I wish them to be, I experience the greatest love possible with my children.

As a teacher, I offer practical information about what is both possible and realistic in a classroom setting. I know the difficulties encountered in the classroom. I know firsthand the seemingly insurmountable challenges a teacher faces in helping a student with AD/HD to succeed. I offer solutions that honor the spirit of the child while meeting his educational needs.

As a spiritual practitioner, I offer insight into the principles that guide us to be the very best parents we can be. These principles are nondenominational and relevant regardless of one's religious beliefs.

By combining these perspectives of parent, teacher, and spiritual counselor, I am able to offer a comprehensive and down-to-earth guide to honoring, nurturing, and loving the AD/HD child. I invite you to embrace the opportunity that is before you now. Working with an AD/HD child, whether at home or in the classroom, gives us the opportunity to develop love and acceptance within ourselves. When we find ourselves frustrated and out of patience, that is the perfect moment to ask, "What is it about me that is reacting so strongly to this child?" In the answers to this question lies the key to our personal transformation. As we transform ourselves, so, too, will our children be transformed.

Acknowledgments

There are many people whose encouragement and support have ensured the publication of this project. I would like to take this opportunity to thank them individually.

I must thank my family. I thank my parents, David Young and Patricia Dewald, for instilling in me the desire to reach my inherent potential; my sisters—Shawn, Sondra, and Amy Young, for insisting that I develop that less serious side of myself; and my grandparents, D. C. and Pauline Young, for always believing in me no matter what. Their support and unconditional love have contributed to this book in countless ways.

Thank you, Mom, for always insisting that someday I would write a book. I know that it was your suggestion that planted the seed for this book.

Without Happy Shaw, I would have spent endless hours in the library and bookstores researching the process of writing and publishing a book. Thank you for your advice, guidance, direction, and support of my project.

Many thanks to Sally Garner for her friendship, encouragement, and endless hours helping me through the editing process.

Dr. Bob Brooks, one of the kindest people I have ever had the privilege to know. Thank you for your generosity and time in reviewing my work and for preparing a fabulous foreword.

I must thank those with whom I have shared my journey of spiritual growth: Reverend Patrick Pollard, Reverend Jack Blackman, Reverend Jennie Goff, Reverend Judy Franks, Marge Larragoite, Karen Richards, Rebecca Allen, Dave Shultz, David Alexander, Barbara Fox, Jeannie Bullard, Judy

Katz, Lynne Curtis, Happy Shaw, and Michelle Taylor. Thank you all for sharing in my journey!

To Greg, I say thank you for your support and encouragement on my spiritual journey as well as your understanding and tolerance of my time spent on this passion of mine.

Finally, to my children, Nickolas, Heather, and Brandi, for providing me with so much writing material. I am honored to be your mother.

1

A New Perspective

Every parent-to-be makes assumptions about the child they will have. Many, if not most of us, assume that our child will be pretty much like other children. We assume that he will be more handsome or more athletic or perhaps more sensitive than most; that she will be uniquely special to the world. We assume that our child will be responsive to our wisdom and our guidance. We assume much.

What we did not assume, nor prepare for, was that our child would become unmanageable at the tender age of two and remain so for years to come. We did not assume that a clean house was a thing of the past. We did not assume that teachers would react to our child with frustration and dismay and that many of them would blame us for that. We could not have prepared for the dread we would feel before the parent-teacher conference. We could not have known that most other children would dislike our child. This was not our dream. We were not prepared for the knot in our stomach that does not leave.

Some parents know from birth that their child is not quite like their friends' children. Others do not notice a problem until sometime after their child begins school. Still others are unaware of the impending disasters until even later. Regardless of when we become aware of the differences in our child, we then begin a journey, which is unknown and incomprehensible to our friends and family. Many of us begin to feel isolated and alienated.

In raising, teaching, and advocating for children with attention deficit/hyperactivity disorder, I have experienced in myself, and observed in others, two extreme approaches, the first being rescue, the second, abandonment.

It is often painful to see our children in the midst of such extremely challenging experiences. Perhaps it is the protective instinct that compels us to free our children from their challenges. Anyone who has served in the capacity of a rescuer knows that we really cannot save them from those challenges. The harder we try, the more it appears to us that they need to be saved. We cannot shelter them from their social and educational bruises any more than we could prevent the inevitable falls when they were learning to walk. Just as some toddlers experience many more falls, our children experience more difficulties.

The other extreme, abandonment, is often seen as a way to allow the child to take his knocks and learn from them. It is a sink-or-swim challenge. We choose this approach only because we ourselves feel helpless and powerless to facilitate the growth of the child. Our children do need to experience the natural consequences of their choices. However, just as most of us would not throw our children into a lake to learn to swim, we cannot throw them into life and truly expect them to figure it all out on their own. Our children need *living* lessons, and we are the instructors.

The biggest challenge in raising and teaching the AD/HD child is not in changing the child, but in changing *our own* thinking, *our* expectations, *our* perceptions, and *our* approach. We must acknowledge that we are the ones with the problem. We do not know how to respond to the child. It means giving up our personal agenda and learning how to respond constructively to the child with AD/HD. The challenge is in knowing when and how to intervene.

Many times we talk about AD/HD children as being *in crisis*. It is important that we differentiate between their crisis and our own. Is the child truly in crisis? Or is it the adults in his life who are in crisis about him? Oftentimes, if we step back and look at the child, he is not experiencing crisis. We are. Sadly, we then go about creating a sense of crisis within the child so that we can convince him of the many changes that must take place. We convince him that he is the root of all of our family problems or problems in the classroom. Eventually, under the weight of such arguments, we can and do create crisis within the child.

It took a long time for me to realize that my son, Nickolas, was not suffering over the fact that his classmates did not like him. He was aware of this, but it did not seem to bother him. It bothered me immensely. It also bothered his teachers. The adults in his life were greatly distressed by his lack of friends; Nickolas was not. Nonetheless, we spent a lot of time and energy trying to convince him that he needed friends, that he wanted friends, that friends were important, that it should bother him that he had no friends, and that *he should change* in order to make friends.

The truth of the matter is that I superimposed pain into his world. It was my pain, my experience, and not his at all. Once I realized that Nickolas was not in crisis because of the number of friends he did or did not have, I released the issue. I discussed it with him only when he brought it up.

Toward the end of the sixth grade, Nickolas began getting referrals to the office for exploding at other children who teased or harassed him in some way. (It is interesting to note here that he was the only one being referred to the office–the antagonists were left to bask in their victory.) Nick's teachers were very much alarmed by his behavior. This explosive behavior was my first indication that the manner in which other kids reacted to him had begun to matter to Nickolas. I could step back and see that he was becoming aware of the interaction with his peers. For the first time, it bothered him when they said mean things about him, and he was out to put a stop to it. He exploded with words, not with violence, so I left it alone for him to come to me.

It was not long until he did. He began to initiate conversations that opened the door to honesty. I allowed him to choose not to deal with the things about himself that fuel the fires in his life, at the same time making it clear that he would eventually need to do so in order to solve the problem. We discussed how many of us put off facing painful things about ourselves for a long time. Most importantly, I let him know that when he is ready and able to look honestly at those things about himself that create conflict in his life, I will be here for him.

Of course, there are situations in which a child is indeed in the midst of crisis. Under such circumstances, our challenge is to remove our own fears and judgments so that our priority is proactive intervention. We must set aside our need to hold this child to our own standards or ideals and instead take on the role of nurturer and healer. Our intention must be to stabilize this child's experience regardless of the cost to our principles. In this process, we gain new insights that cause us to evaluate those ideals that we have held on to for so long.

The child with AD/HD has many challenges to face. We can be grateful for the opportunity to teach our children to be navigators of their own ships. They cannot learn if we do it for them while they play on deck, and they cannot learn if we give them a ship and send them out to sea alone. The only way they can learn is by demonstration and practice. They will, no doubt, get off course at times, but that does not mean the ship will sink. For us, as parents and educators, to teach our children to be navigators of their life means that we will be present when they get off course. We must gently help them to get back on course. We can do this without breaking their spirit. We can honor the spirit within AD/HD children as we promote their learning. It is imperative that we do so. They are future parents, teachers, doctors, clerks, lawyers, mechanics, scientists, secretaries, religious leaders, farmers, managers, politicians, and the like. Inside each of them is a beautiful individual about to blossom. We cannot know what magnificence is within them if we squander it, but we can help them to unfold into their inherent magnificence.

It is our own challenges that disturb us the most. Our needs interfere with our parenting and teaching, and our desires for our children cloud our vision. We must pursue our own personal growth and understanding of our motives in order to be wholly available to these children. They need this more than others do.

I have come to realize that my job parenting children with AD/HD is perhaps as much of a challenge as they face by having the disorder. In order to do an adequate job of raising my children, I have to be committed to seeing clearly where they begin and I end. In addition:

- I must see who they are and not who I wish them to be.
- I must honor the spirit within them and give them only the assistance they need.
- I must relinquish my need to manipulate them into "proper children."
- I must face, and dissolve, my need to reexperience personal issues through my children.
- I must give up the idea that my children somehow scream to the world who *I* am.
- I must give up being embarrassed by their mistakes.
- I must surrender the idea that they need to be "fixed."
- I must enjoy the time I have with them, because we all come to know that the time is too short.

I have read many books on parenting the AD/HD child and many books on parenting in general. From each book I have gleaned understanding, ideas, and insights. I have found for myself and my children that no one approach will work for us. For example, I could not make a commitment to a token system and believe that was *the* answer. I could not be consistent in this approach. Nor could I be consistent with this approach in my classroom.

There are many psychologically sound tools for communicating—intentional dialogue, mirroring, and validation—but I know that I could not make a commitment to always communicating in that way. Sometimes, parents and teachers need to give instructions and have them followed without an in-depth conversation about how the child feels about it. We want to be sensitive to their feelings, but with an AD/HD child, one can quite easily find oneself cornered or frustrated in such a conversation. Our children tend to have a unique perception of the events in their life. Their feelings and perceptions about an event may not be relevant to the situation.

I am finding most of my answers on my own inner journey. I believe the answers are found within each of us; the answer is love. When we learn to honor the spirit of our child, we learn that no *one* technique is the way. Knowing techniques and strategies is important, but it is more important to be guided through our own connection to life, and to realize that our inner voice will tell us how to be in each moment if we learn to hear it.

My daughter Heather is prone to fits of frustration in which she becomes almost hysterical, unable to discuss a situation rationally, calm herself, or to be consoled. It is very frustrating for me as a parent because I feel so helpless and powerless. Recently during one of Heather's episodes, I was able to hear that voice within. I held her in my arms for a moment and reassured her that I knew she would get through this particular challenge and later that evening, she and I would go for a walk together. I felt her relax some and I did follow through with my promise. It was a beautiful evening with a gentle breeze. She chattered about nonsense and we talked about the events of the week. We walked together until she felt complete. I sensed that she had found peace again before suggesting that we call it a night.

Our parenting is affected, in large part, by our own childhood experiences. We are all familiar with the inevitable cycles that flow from generation to generation; our parents raised us the way they were parented, without much hesitation. We may find ourselves repeating those same patterns regardless of our own parenting philosophy. As teachers, we take these learned reactions into our classrooms.

Our generation became aware of the disadvantages to this cyclical approach and began an inquiry into a better way. We have experienced, through the emergence of pop psychology and an emphasis on self-help, a tremendous change in the consciousness of parenting. We have engaged in a process of analyzing our patterns in an effort to understand our own psychological tendencies. We have reviewed our childhood disappointments and traumas in an effort to better understand ourselves and one another. We identified damage that had been done to our young psyches and began displaying the dysfunction of our families of origin; our dysfunctional past became a common topic of conversation. I have come to believe that we are a wounded generation raising children from our own sense of woundedness. Generations past have relied on intuition and a few select parenting resources, such as Dr. Spock. How different we are! Sometimes the simplest decisions cannot be made without conferring with family, friends, professionals, and our children. We have come to make decisions based on popular rhetoric instead of relying upon our own inner guidance system. We have lost faith in our innate ability to determine appropriate courses of action in the best interest of our children.

It is not my intention to downplay the importance of personal growth and discovery—indeed the opposite is true. In order to change instinctive traits, we must make a commitment to personal discovery. My own parenting pitfalls are deeply based in feeling, not in logic or reason. The key to moving beyond those pitfalls is to go beyond the analysis of our childhood wounds to a stage of forgiveness and to cultivate a degree of contentment and peace about what has been, knowing that the past has no power over the present. Through personal healing, we will find a way to reconnect with that within us which already has the answers we seek.

Once I had identified the things I did not like about my own parenting, I seemed helpless to change them. I vowed never to scream at my children. When my children were quite young, I realized that I did yell at them more often than I wanted to. I then seemed to be powerless over my own behavior, yet at the same time, I expected my children to have power over *their* behavior. It was not until I began my own inward journey that I was able to discover and heal the root cause of my tendency to yell.

Each one of us is on a personal journey. Some of us are more deliberate about it than others. I am not suggesting that as the parent or teacher of an AD/HD child, you must run out and enroll in a counseling program. That may be appropriate and it may not. My family sought counseling services for a time and found them to be very beneficial. My own journey now is a spiritual one. I became involved in a spiritual process, which has helped me to unravel my own false beliefs about myself, my definition of God, and my place in the world.

The way I view my children and the way I interact with them has naturally become a part of my inner journey. I have explored who my children are, the nature of their being, their place in the world, and my role in their upbringing. What has unfolded for me is an appreciation of the many variations that nature provides and an appreciation for the uniqueness of my children. There is no shame in the flower that is different from all the rest or is the last to bloom. Nature is not critical of its own creation. Who am I to be critical of my child? Each one of us is born a little different from the rest. Thank goodness this is so. We each bring gifts to share with the world, and we each have issues to work on in life. My children are gifts to me. It is a privilege to watch them grow and learn. They bring many gifts and much delight into my world.

It was not until I could appreciate my own inherent gifts and honor the spirit within myself that I could do so for my children. It was not until I could get beyond the judgment of myself for my "shortcomings" that I could do so for my children. When I learned to see each day as a blessing and an opportunity and I learned to relax and enjoy life, then I could encourage that in my children. When I see spirit looking at me through their eyes, it fills me with joy and I delight in their presence. When I feel spirit, loving me through them, I am filled with appreciation for their unique expression. It is when I lose this connection that I revert to the struggle to coerce them into something they are not. I see my job as nurturing and assisting them in their own self-discovery. I cannot force children to learn lessons they are not yet ready to learn, but I can be observant and prepared to help them when they are ready.

Whatever your perception of God, you can learn to see your child as a product of the most infinite wisdom and intelligence. Your child was not an accident. Your child was not a mistake. Your child was born perfectly himself. This is the starting point. Raising this child is a process of evolution. How he will evolve is only partly up to you. You can enhance his sense of self with support and love, or you can squelch it with criticism and conflict.

I invite you to view your child in a different light. I invite you to consider the possibilities. I suggest that you have nothing to lose by exploring the ideas contained herein and a great deal to gain if they resonate with you. As we explore the different issues we face as parents and teachers of AD/HD children, re-main centered in this truth:

- My child is a unique expression of infinite creativity.
- My child is perfect, whole, and complete in this moment.
- I see spirit expressed through my child.
- I feel the love of God flowing in and through my relationship with my child.
- I am wholly present to offer wisdom and guidance.
- I am wholly present to offer love and support.
- I allow my child to be who he is and I take delight in his presence.
- I allow my child to learn, in her own time, the lessons she must learn.
- I allow spirit to nurture both me and my child in this process.

2

The Diagnosis

What Are the Diagnostic Criteria?

The diagnostic criteria for attention deficit/hyperactivity disorder are defined in the *Diagnostic Statistical Manual IV (DSM-IV)*, the diagnostic tool endorsed by the American Psychiatric Association. The DSM, now in its fourth revision, has changed the terminology used in regards to AD/HD. Many people ask why "hyperactivity" is always included in the name whether or not hyperactivity is present. Before the *DSM* fourth edition was published, the terminology was attention deficit disorder with hyperactivity or attention deficit disorder, undifferentiated type. The *DSM-IV* has termed the disorder attention deficit/hyperactivity disorder and has established the subtypes: *inattentive type, hyperactive/impulsive type,* and *combined type.* Further, in the *DSM-IV,* there have been introduced two separate groups of characteristics to facilitate the differentiation between the subtypes.

The following characteristics must be considered for a diagnosis of AD/HD: inattentive type:

- Often fails to give close attention to details or makes careless mistakes in schoolwork, work, or other activities.

    This describes the child who rushes through his classroom assignments then receives a failing grade

on the assignment because he added instead of sub-
tracting.

- Often has difficulty sustaining attention.
   This is one of the most noticeable characteristics of
   the disorder. It is evident that their attention span is
   much shorter than their peers'.
- Often does not seem to listen when spoken to directly.
   This describes the child who appears to be lost in
   space when spoken to. Often, they will not make
   eye contact and will seem not to notice that anyone
   is speaking to them.
- Often does not follow through on instructions and fails
   to finish tasks.
   If you ask an AD/HD child if he has done something asked of him, a common response might be,
   "Oh, shoot, I forgot." They get excited to begin
   something new then appear to lose interest halfway
   through and never get it finished.
- Often has difficulty organizing tasks and activities.
   This describes the child who cannot seem to get
   started on something because he is unable to do the
   preliminary organizing that must be done in order
   to begin.
- Often avoids dislikes or is reluctant to engage in tasks
   that require sustained mental effort (such as schoolwork and homework).
   The AD/HD child struggles with completing assignments at school and at home, so they eventually exhibit avoidance behaviors.
- Often loses things necessary for tasks or activities.
   This describes the student who loses pencils, pens,
   notebooks, textbooks, house keys, coat, etc.
- Is often easily distracted by extraneous stimuli.
   Most of us can stay focused on an instructor if someone passes by the doorway; the AD/HD child's mind
   is immediately tuned in to extraneous activities. The
   same is true for an interesting toy sitting on a nearby
   shelf; he is unable to concentrate on the task at hand
   because he is consumed by the need to touch the toy.
- Often is forgetful in daily activities.

Routines are hard to establish for these kids. It seems that no matter how many times they repeat a task, they are unable to duplicate the steps without constant reminders. A famous example of this is getting ready to leave for school each morning.

If six or more of these characteristics are rated as "pretty much" or "very much" and are chronic, then a diagnosis of AD/HD: inattentive type is possible.

The second list of characteristics must be considered for a diagnosis of AD/HD: hyperactive/impulsive type.

- Often fidgets with hands or feet or squirms in seat.

    This describes the student who cannot stay seated in a chair. He will change positions constantly, sit on his knees, and get out of his seat to sharpen a pencil over and over again. He will not be able to watch a movie at home without rocking, playing with something nearby, or twiddling his thumbs. He is constantly moving.

- Often leaves seat in classroom or other situations.

    This appears to be caused by the restlessness both of the body and the mind. Sometimes they will have a purpose, such as sharpening that pencil–again, other times they appear to wander aimlessly.

- Often runs about or climbs excessively (in adolescents or adults, may be limited to subjective feelings of rest-lessness).

    Smaller children are often described as climbing the walls or hanging from the ceiling.

- Often has difficulty doing things quietly.

    These children are often unable to work without creating some auditory stimulus. In play, they tend to yell more and be louder than their peers.

- Is often "on the go" or acts as if "driven by a motor."

    Many of these children cannot sit through a story-book at the same age as their peers. They will pass up a snack if they have to sit to eat. They are always running.

- Often talks excessively.

A lot of AD/HD children never stop talking. They do not always have something to say, but they will continue to talk nonetheless.

- Often blurts out answers before the questions are completed.

    This is one of the most significant classroom disruptions from AD/HD children. They have difficulty raising their hand and waiting to be called upon. It seems as though the statement leaves their lips before it enters their mind.

- Often has difficulty awaiting turn.

    These children have significant difficulties in playing games and turn-taking rituals such as conversation. This is often the first significant area of social difficulty.

- Often interrupts or intrudes on others.

    Their behaviors are seen as intrusive by their peers as well as adults. They seem unaware of when a situation or conversation calls for their absence or lack of input. They rarely wait to be invited into a situation, but instead they are seen barging in and trying to take over.

If six of these characteristics are rated as "pretty much" or "very much" and chronic, then a diagnosis of AD/HD: hyperactive/impulsive type is possible. See Appendix A for a checklist.

If both sets of criteria are met, then a diagnosis of AD/HD: combined type is possible.

There is more, however. The *DSM-IV* further stipulates that these characteristics must be present *across settings* and the age of onset must be before the age of seven. AD/HD is a neurobiological disorder that affects a person *in every moment*. If it exists at school, it must also exist at church, Boy Scouts, or home. It may look a little different in each setting, but it is still present regardless of where the person is. This is a disorder that one is born with. It is not something that develops over time or suddenly strikes a person at age nine or nineteen. This is not to say that it must be diagnosed by age seven. This means that when a diagnosis is being considered, the parent can look back in time and remember that as a young child these characteristics were indeed present even if they did not present any real difficulty.

In consideration of the checklists, it is important that we realize that most of us exhibit some of these behaviors or tendencies at times. Some of us may always lose our keys, for example. What differentiates a person with AD/HD is the extent to which these characteristics are present.

My son was diagnosed in the second grade. Even though his younger sister had already been diagnosed, AD/HD never crossed my mind in regard to Nickolas. During the diagnostic process, however, I could easily see how the characteristics were present in kindergarten. The characteristics of AD/HD were immediately seen in the classroom setting, whereas they were not really noticeable at home until later on. Though his kindergarten teacher and I discussed particular areas of concern for Nickolas, at that time they were not overtly problematic. By second grade, they had become problematic, both at school and at home.

On the other hand, I knew from birth that there was something different about my daughter Heather. By the age of three, we were aware that there was definitely a problem. By the age of four, we were in crisis. Unfortunately, a diagnosis for a young child can be more difficult to make. It was not until age ten that we were able to secure a meaningful diagnosis for the complex issues we faced with Heather. At that time, she was diagnosed with depression, AD/HD, and oppositional defiant disorder.

So What Is AD/HD Really?

The person with AD/HD is stimulated by the environment differently than a person without AD/HD. For example, I can walk into a richly stimulating environment and notice that it is very colorful and provides a lot of information. I can make a mental note of that, sit down in the room, and read a book. In a very brief amount of time, I have blocked out the stimulation of the room décor. It is, in no way, a distraction to me. I can come back to it at any time, but it is not holding my attention.

The kid with AD/HD walks into this same room and is immediately turned on to everything in it. He cannot quickly or easily block out, or turn off, the stimulation. He has to take notice of each intricate part of this environment. There is no mechanism for him to choose what he is supposed to pay attention to. He pays attention to all of it. This is fun for him! It is frustrating and even painful for the person insisting he focus in on one particular piece, probably not the one of his choosing.

This is not to say that they cannot ever focus on one thing. They can. When they do, it is usually like tunnel vision. It is very difficult to shift their attention away from the object of attention. They are so focused that they appear to be glued to the activity.

Kids with AD/HD have a very different perception of the environment. They also perceive events and situations uniquely. Because they have difficulty with sequencing, they have difficulty with cause and effect. When little Billy gets punched in the eye, he will stay stuck on having been punched, and he is unable to see how his own actions may have led up to the punch. Fairness for the AD/HD child has only to do with receiving. What they contributed is irrelevant to them.

These kids are oblivious to social clues, so they are unaware of how others are being affected by their actions and how their actions are perceived by others. The talkative kid with AD/HD does not notice when his audience has tired of him and will even seem not to notice when they walk away altogether while he is in midsentence. They seem not to notice when they are being ignored. They also do not "get it" when they are the brunt of the joke. These social nuances develop in early elementary school for most children. They seem not to develop in our kids until middle school.

They are overly sensitive in other situations. When another student bumps him in line, for instance, the AD/HD child will react intensely. He will be positive that it was intentional on the part of the other student. If others laugh at him owing to a funny mistake he has made, he will react with either intense anger or will be intensely insulted and embarrassed. They overreact to many minor situations. One of the first times Nickolas baby-sat his little sister (four at the time), he called me very upset because she had put her dress on backward and refused to turn it around. It took me five minutes to calm him down!

Friendships are rare and fragile. This is primarily due to the AD/HD child's immaturity and inability to perceive and respond to the wants and needs of another person. Typically, they will want to talk about themselves and never want to listen to their friend. They will want to play the games that interest them and will not be interested in a compromise. They will want to take over in a given situation and try to be the one in charge.

They are unable to complete anything from delivering a cup of water to a long-term history project. This is primarily because of the inability to focus on the task at hand and eliminate extraneous stimuli. They can become distracted by the television on their way to get the water. They will procrastinate about the long-term project until a day or two before and somehow believe that they have enough time to get it done.

Their memory seems to fail them often. They have difficulty remembering things they are supposed to do, or the tools necessary to complete the task. They fail to remember rules and routines. They cannot remember to do the same chores each day or write in their assignment notebook each day. They forget to brush their teeth or put on deodorant. They cannot relay a message correctly, if they remember it at all.

They seem to be irresponsible in every way that a person can be irresponsible. They are not typically neat or organized. They can clean their room (which is sure to take days) and then have it destroyed again in ten minutes.

Has This Condition Always Existed?

I am often asked when AD/HD "began." What about in the forties and fifties? What about a hundred years ago? While the name has changed many times, AD/HD has always existed.

At the turn of the twentieth century, children who exhibited the characteristics of AD/HD were said to have a *defect in moral character.* Later in the century, it was termed *minimal brain dysfunction.* The second edition of the *DSM,* during the mid-1900s, identified the characteristics of this disorder as the *hyperkinetic reaction to childhood,* which completely missed the ADD child without hyperactivity. During the seventies, it became evident that there were children without hyperactivity who exhibited many of the other characteristics. In 1980, with the third edition of the DSM, the disorder became known as *attention deficit disorder.* With further scientific advances, the disorder became redefined as *Attention Deficit/Hyperactivity Disorder* later in that decade.

Whatever the label, the characteristics have always been the same. It is we, as a society, who are different. The world is a different place with vastly different expectations placed on kids today that were not there only a couple of generations ago.

One primary difference that affects children with AD/HD is the expectation of college. A hundred years ago, our country was primarily agricultural. When a particular child did not do well in school, especially a boy, he would return home to work with his father sooner than other students. In the forties and fifties there were many career opportunities that did not require higher education and allowed a man to earn a good living, support his family, and save for retirement.

My family has a history of railroaders. Certainly, no college degree was required. The pay and benefits were top-notch. School success or failure mattered very little, if at all. My father wanted to be a fireman. Again, no college degree was required. He knew that he needed to graduate from high school, which could be done with a D average. My grandparents' goal for him was to graduate from high school. Had he jeopardized that goal, they would have sternly corrected his course. However, his foolishness in school and his low grades were not much of a bother to them; they simply wanted their kids to finish high school. All five of them did, and two of them attended college to become a teacher and a nurse. My father has enjoyed a long and prosperous career with the railroad.

Research has found a definite genetic correlation in AD/HD. By asking questions of your family about characteristics, not labels, you are likely to find some AD/HD in your lineage. My father has expressed curiosity about the possibility of having the disorder himself. One of my three sisters was diagnosed with ADD in the 1980s. Another sister I would bet a brand-new copper penny on.

Today, there are few career opportunities, even with a college degree, that offer the kind of stability that was the norm earlier in the century. It is difficult to earn a living without a college degree. We have had to work very hard to make our way in life but many of us do not feel that our retirement years are secured. We are uncertain about the future of our own generation and we are certainly uncertain about the future of our children's generation. What we do know is that it is a competitive world out there where those with the degrees get the highest-paying jobs. We know that luck will not get our kids far. We know that their high school grade point average matters so they can attend a good college, do well there, earn a good degree, secure a good career for themselves. At least we think we know these things.

If we look realistically at the situation, we can see that we are afraid for our children. We hear it in the news and in our daily conversations. We live with uncertainty for our future and we fear what the future may hold for our children. We are afraid of their failure in school because we now equate a lack of school success with failure in the adult world. We assume that a D student cannot and will not achieve as an adult. As a result of our own fears, we are now placing much higher demands and expectations on our children. Because of these higher expectations, we have set the stage for despondency for many of our children who have AD/HD.

The time has come for us to deal with our own fears and to stop imposing our fears onto our children. This is not to say that we should not encourage school success. It is to say, however, that we need always to be in touch with *why* it is so important to *us* that they achieve a certain level of success. We must remember that what we want for our children and what they choose for themselves will sometimes differ.

I consulted with a parent of a young girl who had recently been diagnosed with Attention Deficit/Hyperactivity Disorder: inattentive type. Sheila was somewhat relieved when the psychologist who evaluated her daughter explained to her that Desiree had AD/HD. Though apprehensive, she was also looking forward to the first medication trial and anticipating good results. We met and reviewed Desiree's school records. Desiree was failing several subjects and the school was recommending retention. Sheila was confused and unsure of what was best for Desiree at this point. We arranged for Desiree not to be retained in the sixth grade and scheduled a meeting with her teachers to implement an appropriate intervention plan for her. Sheila called the day before our scheduled meeting, overwhelmed by Desiree's response to the medication and to the idea of special accommodations in the classroom. Desiree did not like taking the medication and refused to take it anymore. She also declared that she did not need any special interventions at school, did not want to attend the scheduled meeting, and would refuse to follow any program whatsoever. Sheila's response was admirable. She canceled the meeting at the school and scheduled a meeting with the psychologist. She sat Desiree down and explained her disappointment in Desiree's choices. Then, she outlined the natural consequences of those choices. Sheila explained that with no interventions in place, based on the first six months of the school year, it was quite likely that her grades would not improve, and because she was refusing to receive help, she would be retained if she continued to fail. Sheila left the decision up to Desiree. Within a few days, Desiree had changed her mind. We met with her teachers and wrote a 504 Accommodation Plan. The psychologist began a new medication trial with her. For the remainder of the school year, she continued to show improvement.

Sheila had been afraid that if Desiree failed the sixth grade, she would then be bored repeating the same curriculum, her self-esteem would suffer and she would experience social stigma. All of these fears are understandable. Sheila released her fears about Desiree's failure and accepted the fact that ultimately Desiree herself had to make some difficult decisions. Because Sheila was able to surrender to the possibilities, the outcomes will be more meaningful to both of them.

Faith is an important component to being able to allow our children the freedom to choose for themselves how important school success is for them. We must develop a deep, abiding faith that the universe is not going to abandon our children; that, in fact, the universe has not abandoned us. I encourage you to know that the one Ultimate Power in the universe is infinite in wisdom and intelligence and that our children are safe in their world. We can no longer afford to communicate our fears to them that their world is not a safe place.

Affirmation: I relax into the Divine Presence that lovingly provides for me and my child. Knowing that I am safe in the world, I have faith and confidence that my child is supported today and always by a Power that is greater than I am. I release all fears for _____ 's future success and allow him to be and become just the way that he needs to. I am wholly available to support his growth.

How Do I Know It Really Is AD/HD?

There are other conditions and situations that can look like AD/HD, so it is imperative that you have a knowledgeable and thorough physician to work with. Many fine doctors know little about this disorder. Those who do not have a particular interest or specialty in AD/HD may not be aware of the continuously evolving and changing information regarding the disorder and its treatment. Find a professional who is truly qualified to evaluate and diagnose AD/HD. Some pediatricians have practices with a high concentration of AD/HD clientele; others do not. In some cases, it is necessary to have an evaluation performed by a qualified mental health professional. Regardless of what credentials a professional has, it is important that he or she is aware of the most recent advances in AD/HD research and can provide a comprehensive evaluation.

Environmental concerns should be considered, as major life changes or stresses can cause a child to exhibit many AD/HD behaviors. Other biological conditions have some of the same characteristics as well.

AD/HD may also coexist with another condition. It then becomes difficult to separate the two. AD/HD, when present with another condition, is a secondary condition. The best professional information I have is that the "comorbid condition" (the *other* condition) should be treated first. For example, if a person is diagnosed with AD/HD and depression, the depression—as the primary condition—should be adequately addressed before the AD/HD can be attended to. Not all professionals take this approach and they may not be wrong for not doing so, but this is an approach that has been presented by leading professionals in this field and is the one that makes the most sense to me.

Heather was treated for AD/HD for several years before I became aware that the worst of her behavior fit the criteria for childhood depression. We had tried many different medications and combinations, some of which made her behavior worse. We eventually eliminated all of the treatment for the AD/HD and began treating her depression with Prozac. We subsequently found we did not need to treat the AD/HD with medication. This may change tomorrow, but for today, we are medically treating the symptoms of depression only. Meanwhile, she is still being observed for the possibility of other conditions.

There is one thing I am absolutely certain of: If you have a child with extreme difficulties, you want the very best diagnosis and treatment available. If you think that your child may have AD/HD, make an appointment with an experienced physician who will provide a comprehensive evaluation. I think it is a mistake for a physician to issue a diagnosis of AD/HD and write a prescription based on a fifteen-minute appointment. I think it is a mistake to try a stimulant medication to see if it works and base a diagnosis on the outcome of the medication trial. Talk with your doctor about a thorough evaluation. Even if you feel the situation is desperate, insist upon a comprehensive evaluation.

This can be difficult for a parent to do because, when our child is suffering, we want relief for them and for ourselves. A friend who is a pediatrician tells me that a lot of parents do not want a comprehensive evaluation. They want a prescription. They want immediate relief. If you find yourself to be one of these parents, let me assure you that there is no instant relief. Even if your child responds well to medication, this only makes the disorder easier to manage and you will soon realize that you are still dealing with the very same issues.

I have seen this many times in my role as teacher and as advocate. I see parents in crisis, desperate for a solution to their problems. They get an evaluation and a prescription. They are overjoyed by the miraculous results offered by the medication. "It's like having a whole new kid." They begin to think that everything has become *normal*. They do not attend support meetings anymore and they do not monitor their child as closely. I refer to this as the honeymoon period. It will pass. Suddenly, they will find themselves back in crisis, wondering why the medication is no longer working. In reality, the medicine *is* still working. The child *is* performing better. However, the medication has not changed the fact that this child has AD/HD. We acclimate to the improvements and find ourselves facing the same issues.

Having a child with AD/HD requires a team effort toward success. With a qualified professional on your team, you are empowered to make significant milestones with your child. Regardless of how you choose to treat the diagnosis, it is imperative that you have the very best medical advice available and an ongoing relationship with a professional who can assist you as your needs change along the way.

3

Treating AD/HD

What Medical Treatments Are Available?

Medication is a difficult issue. Whether or not to medicate a child is one of the most difficult decisions a parent will ever have to face. There are many factors that must be considered. For some of us, the diagnosis alone is a challenge. The stigma of Ritalin and other stimulant drugs used to treat AD/HD has become so strong that it can be a source of embarrassment for some. I have struggled with the question, "By medicating my child, am I giving him the message that he is not okay the way he is?" Many parents wonder if the medication will become a crutch for their child. Some are concerned with the issue of addiction and dependency. The issue of stunted growth surfaces as well.

The stigma of both the diagnosis of AD/HD and the pharmacological treatment of AD/HD can be overwhelming to any parent confronted directly with the issue. It is true that there are a lot of kids being diagnosed with AD/HD. It is possible that we are too quick to rush to judgment and refer these kids for evaluation. It is possible that too many physicians are passing out the diagnosis too quickly and it is possible that they are too quick to prescribe medication. What we know, regardless of the overdiagnosis controversy, is that AD/HD is a real, identifiable, and treatable neurobiological condition. For people who do not believe in AD/HD, I invite them to try to raise a child who has it.

Regardless of the possibility of overdiagnosis and overmedication of children, our challenge, as parents, is to disregard the stigma. We must determine what is true for *our* child. It is possible that there are many children misdiagnosed as having AD/HD. This is not my concern. My concern is my child's diagnosis and my child's treatment.

I have chosen to medicate my children. My feelings about medication have fluctuated and I have been ambivalent. Many changes have been made in their medication regimen over the years, including its discontinuation altogether when it did not appear to be working. I have worried about the message I am giving my children and have agonized over whether or not I am telling them that they are not okay just the way they are, that they need a pill to be okay.

At one of CHADD's annual conferences, I had a near panic attack. I realized that I had never asked my son if he wanted to take the medication. He had never been given the option. Never had I asked him what message he was receiving. I then decided he was old enough to be involved in this decision. To my relief, he wanted to remain on the medication; the medication helps him feel "more like himself." It allows him to make better choices and have greater control over who he is. It does not make him feel that he is not okay. It makes him feel that he *is* okay.

At some point, he may decide that he no longer wants to take the medication. I intend to allow him that choice. I made the choice for him when he was too young to make the choice for himself. He has been given an opportunity to experience himself with the medication, and the freedom to be the very best he can be.

I will always provide feedback for him and make my recommendations, but his process may necessitate a time without meds. I must honor the spirit within him by allowing him the opportunity to choose for himself when he is of an age to do so. Should he decide he needs a trial off medication, I will establish very clear expectations and consequences prior to such a trial. Not having the benefit of the medication because he chose not to take it will not change my expectations of him.

Medication can provide an individual with AD/HD an opportunity to experience greater self-control and expression. Many times, I hear the argument that medication is a crutch. We do not deny a crutch to a child with a broken leg. We do not deny the child with asthma an inhaler. We provide our children with what they need to be healthy, happy, and successful individuals. If medication for AD/HD can provide a child with these opportunities, then there can be nothing wrong with doing so.

Each parent has to make these decisions based on what is best for their child and their family. We can choose to medicate our children and honor them for who they are. We can do so by providing them an opportunity to be successful with the assistance of medication. We can also see their individual talents. We can choose not to medicate our children and to provide them with other tools to manage their behavior and feel good about themselves. It is a personal journey and a choice that must be made within the stillness of our own soul.

The issue of addiction and dependency has been put to rest time and time again. However, until you are faced with the issue, you may be unaware of the facts. The medications used to treat AD/HD are short-lived in the body and are not addictive or habit-forming. They also do not increase the likelihood of drug and alcohol abuse, and if anything, decrease these risks. There are many studies available to alleviate any concerns you may have about addiction and dependency. If you are concerned about dependency issues, ask your doctor to direct you to these studies.

It was once thought that the use of a stimulant medication would stunt a child's growth. People who chose to medicate their children with stimulants would often take them off the medication in the summer months so they could grow. This issue still surfaces today. One of my students was taken off medication completely because his family and his doctor were concerned about his growth, even though both of his parents were small people. The unfortunate result was that a struggling student on medication became an unmanageable student without it. Research has proven that children who take stimulant medications do, in fact, reach their inherent growth potential. Again, if this is a particular concern of yours, talk with your doctor.

If you decide to medicate your child, know that it is a process like anything else. There are several different medications that are commonly used. There are different combinations of medications commonly used to meet the needs of individuals. It may take trials of several different medications in various dosages and combinations before you find the right medication(s) and the right dosage. Having a physician that you trust is imperative. As your child grows and matures, dosages will need to be adjusted. This is the same principle as with Tylenol. A baby gets a tiny dose of Tylenol compared to what you may take for a headache. It is no different with any prescription medication. The dosage of Ritalin, or any medication used to treat AD/HD, will need to be adjusted periodically because your child is growing. You may be the first to notice that your child's current dosage does not seem to be as effective as it once was.

How Does the Medication Work?

The most widely prescribed medications for AD/HD are stimulants, Ritalin and Dexedrine being the most common. Ritalin and Dexedrine have a proven track record of safety and effectiveness. Cylert has also been used, however it has recently been restricted due to liver toxicity. Adderall is a fairly new addition that has received positive reviews from physicians and patients alike.

It is scary for some parents to think of giving their child a stimulant because many people think of stimulants primarily as recreational drugs. If I were to take the amount of Dexedrine that my twelve-year-old, seventy-five-pound son takes, I would be a mess. My heart, my body, and my mind would be racing. Stimulant medications have been found to have the opposite effect on a child with AD/HD.

To understand the effectiveness of a stimulant on an individual with AD/HD, it is important to understand the basic theory of the disorder. Our brains are full of messengers called neurotransmitters. They take information from one place to another. Through an elaborate process, which depends upon these neurotransmitters, we are able to make decisions about how we will behave. In the brain with AD/HD, these neurotransmitters are slower; the messages do not get transmitted quickly enough. It is this lag that causes our children to act before they think about it. The message that their actions are inappropriate does not get there in time to stop the action. Their decision-making ability is delayed because of these slow-moving neurotransmitters. The stimulant speeds up the neurotransmitters in the brain, enhancing the child's ability to slow down, focus, think things through, and behave in a more acceptable manner.

Are There Side Effects to the Medication?

Perhaps the biggest deterrent to medication is the concern about side effects. These vary and are usually mild to moderate in nature. I divide side effects into two categories: those I can live with, and those I cannot. There are enough medications out there to be tried that I am not willing to continue a medication with unacceptable side effects.

The first medication we tried with my son affected his mood. Nickolas seemed to be frustrated more easily and he cried a lot more. Even with changes to the dosage, this effect continued. We discontinued that particular medication and began a new medication trial. Other side effects that I am not willing to tolerate are headaches, nausea, dizziness, negative personality changes, tics, and sleeplessness. I can only ask my child to take medications that make him feel *better*.

A decrease in appetite is a side effect that we do live with. Nickolas is able to get down a good breakfast before the decrease in appetite and by 4:00 P.M. he is starving. The challenge is in having him eat lunch, eat a balanced diet, and not allow him to load up on junk between 4:00 P.M. and dinnertime. Some kids are on a continuous dose and may not experience the 4:00 P.M. feeding frenzy, in which case, decreased appetite may present more of a problem.

Constipation is another side effect we have dealt with. It has been a simple issue for us. A stool softener, taken before bedtime, with a glass of water has been a simple way of combating this irritating side effect.

Each medication seems to interact somewhat differently with each child and other side effects may be encountered. It is important that we monitor our children closely while trying a new medication or an adjusted dosage for any side effects that may be present. Only you and your child can determine if a medication is working or not. Always ask yourself, "Does this medication enhance my child's sense of self-worth and self-control?" If the answer is yes, you are probably on the right track. If the answer is no, then alert your physician and reevaluate your treatment approach.

Sarah's son Brandon had been taking stimulant medication for several years when he began to develop tics. Tics are involuntary movements such as snorting or twitching. Brandon's tics increased in severity very quickly until he was unable to control the movement of his head. Sarah's doctor assured her that these tics were not caused by the medication. Brandon was given medications to help with the loss of muscle control and a referral to a neurologist, who immediately diagnosed him with Tourette's syndrome. It was after this shocking diagnosis with a depressing prognosis that Sarah decided to take Brandon off the stimulant medication. It was a difficult decision because the medication had proven so effective for Brandon. However, within days, the tics began to subside and eventually disappeared altogether.

Should I Medicate My Child During the Summer?

Sometimes parents choose to take their children off medication during the summer months. Whether or not this is a good idea depends on your personal situation. If you are home with your child during the summer months, you may choose not to medicate. If your child is in a summer program that he can be successful in without medication, again you may choose not to medicate. Most of the time, our children are more successful both at home and in summer programs if they continue to take their medication. I suggest parents base their decisions on facts and personal experience rather than on rhetoric and rumor. There are no medical advantages to the withdrawal of treatment for the summer months.

What About Alternative Treatments?

Because medicating our children is such a difficult decision, many of us have looked into alternative treatment methods. There is nothing wrong with alternative medicine, but there is no proven method of alternative treatment for AD/HD.

I caution parents not to make decisions out of fear and desperation. We have tried alternative treatments including dietary changes, megadoses of supplements, herbal and homeopathic remedies, and chiropractic. For a time, I was very susceptible to the claims of others regarding alternative treatments for AD/HD. I was desperate for a cure so I was ready to try expensive and radical treatments. None of them cured my children. Some of them helped. One helped significantly, though not permanently. The end result of my trials is that I have spent a lot of money on things that have no scientific basis and ultimately were not helpful for my child.

I believe that every product will help some people, but that no single product will help all children with AD/HD. If you choose to try alternative treatments, be realistic about the outcome. Know that the likelihood of success is minimal. Also know there are no alternative treatments on the market that are proven to be effective for individuals with AD/HD, regardless of their claims. There are also no alternative treatments, to my knowledge, that have even been studied extensively for use as treatment of AD/HD. Be aware that the claims made by many representatives for alternative treatments are based solely on testimonials and not on scientific studies. You must also be careful about combining alternative treatments with medication. There usually are no studies of drug interactions on alternative substances. Always consult your doctor before combining treatments!

AD/HD is a hot issue right now. Every company wants a piece of this pie. I caution parents not to allow salesmen, well-intentioned or not, to take advantage of you in a time of emotional vulnerability. These people offer tales of miraculous recoveries for kids with AD/HD. Some even resort to guilt tactics and imply that if you really care for your child, you will bear the financial burden of trying their product. Many of them will provide you with written testimonials and studies they feel should lead you to a conclusion that their product is safe and effective for the treatment of AD/HD. I encourage you to ask them to provide you with copies of the credible, scientific studies done on their product as it pertains specifically to the treatment of Attention Deficit/Hyperactivity Disorder. Most likely, no such studies exist.

Whatever decision we make regarding the medical treatment of our AD/HD child, it is of utmost import that we are at peace with our decision. We make the best judgments we can and we cannot afford to place undue value on the opinions of others. There are a variety of treatment options available and we must become educated about our many options. We must trust ourselves to know what is best for our child.

Affirmation: As I attempt to make the best treatment decisions for my child, I quiet my mind, tune out the opinions and advice of others, and seek guidance from within.

4

Life at Home

Life at home for the family of an AD/HD child can be quite humorous. I sometimes feel as if my family is a chaotic and frustrated mess. Regardless of the time of year, we always have a lot going on. Families that include an AD/HD child are faced with issues that other families are not faced with. It is good to see ourselves in a humorous light. Otherwise, we may crumble under the weight of it all.

In order to maintain a healthy family atmosphere, it is important that we recognize the many aspects of our life and develop an appreciation for our special situation. We must carefully guard against the tendency to be crisis-oriented. Crisis-oriented families are typically reactive instead of proactive. Support groups can offer valuable assistance and resources necessary to achieve a balanced home life in spite of our challenges. Often, there are advocacy organizations available to provide assistance in developing appropriate educational interventions. This type of assistance drastically reduces the emotional strain imposed on families with AD/HD children. We may sometimes feel as though we are facing these important issues alone as we perceive that our spouse may be unable to support us in some of our endeavors. And it is always a challenge to make time for our marriage since it is so easy to become absorbed in the issues we are confronted with. Some of us are truly facing these issues alone, without the benefit of a spouse and others must do so while adjusting to a blended family.

There are grandparents raising their grandchildren and aunts and uncles raising their nieces and nephews. Most of us encounter issues with our extended families as we make decisions about the treatment and interventions available for our children. Those of us with more than one child must take on the role of referee between our children. And finally, when we are at our wit's end and attempt to "get away from it all" by going on vacation, that too becomes a challenge. We return to daily life once again attempting to achieve balance and harmony. With so many unique family considerations, it is important to take time to develop an appreciation for the peculiarity of our lives.

The Crisis-Oriented Family

It is too easy to become a family in crisis. This is an issue that I have dealt with in my own family. I have also dealt with this issue as a teacher and as the chapter coordinator for the local CHADD chapter. Families dealing with AD/HD have a tendency to become crisis-oriented. This is dangerous and counterproductive to building a loving, supportive family and to confronting the issues faced by all individuals with Attention Deficit/Hyperactivity Disorder.

Most families experience crises before and at the time of the diagnosis. Most of us are led to an evaluation because of a crisis. The diagnosis itself can initiate crisis with all of the controversy surrounding AD/HD, the psychological, medicinal, and educational implications to be considered, and the permanency of the diagnosis. A diagnosis of AD/HD generates an array of other issues to be dealt with. It also offers relief to many because finally there is an explanation for the difficulties they have encountered and possibilities for treatment. During this phase, parents typically seek an exchange of information and support with those in similar situations. They are relieved to find other parents working with the same issues.

Once the initial storm passes, there is often a return to some semblance of normalcy. I have observed, time and time again, that many families have a tendency to take a break from the consumption of information and support. They may not read any new information, the newest issue of *Attention!* magazine may go unread, the support group meeting goes unattended, and the maintenance visits to the psychologist are canceled. Everything at home seems to be okay, so they take a break from the issue of AD/HD.

Because the diagnosis of AD/HD is a permanent one, the issues resurface. The family experiences upheaval and chaos once again and they enter into a new phase of crisis. During this period, family members will reach out for support. They will call the local CHADD line and request that their phone calls be returned immediately. They will call their psychologist and request an immediate appointment. They will desperately try to find a program that will work with their child *today* and will become angry if none is available.

The support *is* available. Someone probably will return the call from the local support group and talk for a long while. The doctor or psychologist will fit them in for an immediate visit. Things will settle down again. The crisis will diminish.

Then the cycle is repeated. You can see how easy it is to fall into this pattern. There are always going to be times when everything seems to be normal or under control and times when everything is topsy-turvy and we think we are going to fall apart. The issue of raising a child with AD/HD is ever-present whether things are under control or not.

We cannot afford to be crisis-oriented because the more we are, the more crises we will experience. We must come to understand and accept that even if today was a very good day, tomorrow may hold all of the turmoil we can imagine. Even though the report from school was good this week, it may be terrible on Monday. We cannot afford to ignore this issue in our life because things are going well. The crisis-oriented family is reactive. They react the same way to a negative situation as they acted the time before. They are not proactive. They do not take the necessary steps to respond differently the next time a situation arises.

It is important to consider the potential impact that this has on our children. What do we teach them by being crisis-oriented? What is the model for them as they see us take action only out of desperation? What is the message when they see us react so strongly to situations as they arise? Do we want to teach our children to respond in this way?

To avoid being a crisis-oriented family, we must make a commitment to a maintenance approach to the issues present in our family. If AD/HD is an issue, we must make a commitment to effectively deal with it daily. This is not to say that we should live, eat, and breathe Attention Deficit/Hyperactivity Disorder. It does not have to be the focus of our every moment. We should, however, be willing to work with the issues daily. We must be willing to evaluate what went well on a good day and what did not go well on a not-so-good day. We must be willing to keep maintenance appointments with our pediatricians and therapists. We must be willing to attend meetings or appointments that will offer valuable information and support. We must be proactive instead of reactive. Most importantly, we must keep a balanced perspective of what is really important in life.

Support Groups

I cannot say enough about support groups. A family faced with the issues of AD/HD has a lot to gain from attending one. I feel it is also important that we have something to give at these meetings. It is the *exchange* of information and support that is invaluable. When I need support, I am grateful that there are other parents present to provide it, and I experience a sense of satisfaction when I can contribute support for someone else in need. It is validating to hear that other parents of AD/HD children are experiencing the same difficulties you are. It is reassuring to hear success stories from the people who came to share them, when everything is good at their house today. We have much to gain from one another's experiences and knowledge. It is a mistake to ignore this resource.

Take advantage of your local support group as often as possible, even if you are not currently experiencing a crisis in your life. The information you receive will be relevant at some point. If you have an opportunity to hear a lecture by a qualified expert on AD/HD, you will glean insight from what that expert has to say and that insight will help you in the future. Being present for such lectures also demonstrates to the professional that his time and expertise are appreciated. This encourages him and others to continue to donate their time and effort on our behalf.

It is in the best interest of our children that we continue to build greater and greater resources with which to confront the issues in their life. As a community, we can precipitate changes in the perceptions and practices in our schools if we join together to do so. We cannot effect change on a large scale if we do not work together.

CHADD is a national organization that provides information, support, and advocacy for those affected by Attention Deficit/Hyperactivity Disorder. There are local chapters worldwide. Most provide qualified experts to speak about relevant issues. Most provide an opportunity for parents to support one another through open discussions. Many are involved in the community to effect change. Most of these benefits are free of charge. A family membership for the national organization is inexpensive and comes with benefits that far outweigh the cost. I have been involved with CHADD for many years.

Family life is greatly enhanced when we know that we are not alone. When we discuss with other parents, siblings, teachers, counselors, and individuals with AD/HD the issues that are relevant in our lives, we are met with compassion and understanding. We also find realistic, solution-oriented suggestions. We arm ourselves to better cope with the issues in our lives and to bring about positive changes. Talking with other parents who understand our circumstances allows us to release our frustration, blame, and self-neglect in a safe environment.

The Nonsupportive Spouse

There are many families in which the two parents do not see eye to eye on the issues of Attention Deficit/Hyperactivity Disorder as they relate to their child. This creates a great deal of emotional strain on the entire family. When there is a lack of agreement on what approach to take in raising a child, the resulting confusion can add to the existing difficulties.

Often one parent pursues an evaluation for the child without the support of the spouse. Typically, though not always, it is the mother who initiates the process. When a diagnosis is given, the parent who initially pursued the evaluation is anxious to share the answers with her spouse. It is disheartening to find that her spouse is resistant to the information she has to share. One parent may feel that there is nothing wrong with the child—she just needs more discipline, more love, or better teachers. This spouse may not be willing to look at the characteristics of AD/HD as being relevant to his child. This parent may also refuse to entertain the possibility of medication. This leaves the other parent feeling as though he or she is unable to appropriately care for the child. It creates a stalemate. No one can move. No one can provide the necessary intervention for the child, and the child continues to struggle.

There are also situations in which both parents can agree to the existence of AD/HD, but cannot agree to the best approach to dealing with the many issues raised in relation to the diagnosis. Discipline is the primary source of disagreement. Many times, one parent will feel that more discipline, which usually means harsher punishments, is what is necessary to overcome the difficulties of AD/HD.

There are disagreements on many other issues such as medication, responsibility, homework, and communicating with the schools. This, too, leads to increased confusion and decreased consistency for the child.

One spouse may make a commitment to a consistent method or philosophy of training without the other's support or participation. In this situation, the parent making the commitment will likely become exhausted with the attempt to carry on alone. This parent may also become resentful and tension will certainly follow.

Regardless of the specific nature of the disagreements, if you are a parent with a plan and you feel that your partner does not support or participate in your plan, this is undoubtedly a serious issue in your family.

Each of us must do what we feel is best for our child. With or without the support of our spouse, we can honor the spirit of our children by accepting them for who they are, helping them to unfold as the wonderful beings they already are, and sharing our unconditional love and support with them. This is your gift to your child. It does not cost anything and it lasts a lifetime.

The most important thing you can do is give yourself a break. Acknowledge that it would be easier if you had a like-minded partner in the endeavor and accept the fact that today you do not. Do the best you can. When you fall short of your goals and intentions, do not beat yourself up. Take a break and then begin again. It is also important to build a support network of people you can confide in who support you in your efforts.

Always remember that efforts to change your spouse will most likely be futile. It is more important to remain focused on your own commitment. My theory is if what I do works, others will eventually see that it works and will join me in my endeavors. If they do not, I can at least say that I have done my personal best.

Nurturing Your Marriage

Regardless of our disagreements, we must continue to nurture our marriage. It is no secret that divorce rates are very high. There are intense challenges confronting every marriage. We must not let the issue of AD/HD create an impassable obstacle in our marriage. We must also guard against becoming so consumed by the issues presented by this disorder that we fail to take the time to care for our relationship.

It is often difficult for parents of a child with AD/HD to find child care. Our children are more of a challenge than the average baby-sitter is up for. We must be persistent in our search for sitters. We must make time for ourselves; time for the two of us to be alone. It is important to have a date, to go to movies, to spend time alone together.

If child care is a difficult issue for your family, begin combing your community service organizations in search of respite care. Respite care is a service provided to address this very need. Qualified, trained individuals will be sent to your home to care for your children occasionally so that you may enjoy some time away. Locating this service may require some research time and patience. Public social service agencies such as the Children, Youth, and Families Department may be able to point you in the right direction. Most support and/or advocacy organizations will also have referral information. This is a common service provided to foster care providers, so contacting agencies that provide services for those families should be beneficial.

Sometimes, the issues about our child are so pressing that we find it difficult to leave room for anything else. We must get past this. We must agree to leave the issues for a time and enjoy each other's company. It is important to spend time alone together to remind us why it is that we *are* together. We have to be reminded that our relationship is not just about raising children and paying bills. Even when we cannot get away, we must sneak some time together whether it is after the children have gone to bed or while they play outside. We have to enjoy each other and forget, for a time, all that we are dealing with.

If at all possible, I highly recommend out-of-town vacations without the children. This is a rare and golden opportunity for a couple to escape the day-to-day responsibilities of their life together. Greg and I once had a wonderful four-day vacation to Seattle while my mother stayed with the kids. We took a cruise, went whale watching, and had nothing to do but enjoy each other's company. It was fabulous. It allowed us to be together romantically without the business of the life we have built together. We were reminded why it is that we chose to build a life together in the first place.

The Single Parent with an AD/HD Child

Being the parent of an AD/HD child is a difficult job even with a supportive spouse. Being a single parent is a difficult job in and of itself. For those single parents with a child who has AD/HD, this is double duty. It is important to have a network of friends and family to provide needed support. Attending and becoming involved in a support group is a valuable resource. It is helpful to find other supportive adults to be present and to offer needed breaks. There are support groups for single parents in addition to those for parents of children with AD/HD. There is no doubt that people faced with both issues will be present in either group.

These groups often sponsor parent-child activities, outings that provide an opportunity for you and your child to engage in group activities. Many have found that the presence of other single-parent families decreases feelings of anxiety and alienation.

Blended Family Issues

Families joined together with existing children face their own unique challenges. No doubt, the presence of AD/HD within a stepfamily is an additional burden. Greg and I met when Nickolas was three years old. At that time, we had no idea that Nickolas had AD/HD. We were fortunate that Greg and Nickolas had developed a close relationship prior to the time Nickolas's AD/HD became a problem. We encountered the typical family issues and did not have additional problems due to the stepparent relationship. We were very fortunate. This is not the case for many families.

Many times, there is no genuine parent-child relationship to begin with. If it is difficult for a parent to accept the AD/HD child as he is, it may be even more difficult for a stepparent to do so. The parent who is taking primary responsibility for the treatment of AD/HD must communicate, in many cases, with both the natural parent and the stepparent. If met with resistance from both parties, the resulting anxiety can be overwhelming.

The natural parent is in the unfortunate position of making decisions that may seem ludicrous or incomprehensible to her partner. The natural parent must educate the spouse about AD/HD and attempt to evoke empathy, compassion, and understanding for their child. The job of a stepparent is not an easy one. The exposure to different perspectives and support from others in similar situations found at a support group may prove to be quite valuable. Counseling with a therapist experienced in working with both AD/HD and blended family issues can also help to build a healthy family climate.

It is crucial to have unconditional support for the choices we make regarding our children. If we do not have this support from our spouse, we must make sure that we have it from another source. We must remain firm in our foremost commitment to our children.

Extended Family Issues

There is much to be gained from the support of our extended family. When we receive their encouragement and support, we have more strength and determination to do the things we must do. Without this support, we are at a distinct disadvantage.

It can be difficult for our families to understand why our children behave the way they do. I often hear of grandparents who believe their own children are failures as parents and are the cause of their grandchild's difficulties. I hear accounts of adult siblings, whose children do not have AD/HD, offering criticism and advice for the parent of an AD/HD child. This type of resistance increases the feelings of alienation often experienced by parents of AD/HD children. There are stories of families literally torn apart by the existence of AD/HD.

Many times Grandma and Grandpa will no longer allow the children to sleep over or visit without Mom and Dad. Other grandchildren are favored over the AD/HD grandchild. Painful comparisons are made. Sadly, divisions are made within the extended family.

It is important to educate our family about Attention Deficit/Hyperactivity Disorder. We can provide them with credible information about the existence and treatment of the disorder. We can explain to them the reasoning behind our decisions. We can attempt to make them understand that what we are doing is the very best for our children. If they do not perceive the information you present verbally as being credible, it may be wise to provide some written materials. I believe that most families are available to offer support and understanding, but we must evaluate how we can protect the best interests of our children and have a loving and beneficial relationship with our family. The answer is different for each family.

Regardless of the position taken by members of our extended family, we are confronted by an important issue in our child's life. We have made, and will continue to make, the best decisions that we can for our children and our family. It is not imperative that our extended family support our decisions. It is imperative that our children receive acceptance and love from their family.

Raising Someone Else's Child

Raising a child with AD/HD is an enormous task. There are those who, for one reason or another, are raising a child who is not their biological son or daughter. There are occasions where a child is being raised by his grandparents or his aunt and uncle.

Under such circumstances, it may be beneficial for the caregiver to access several different sources of support. In addition to the issues presented by the disorder, there are the fundamental issues presented to those raising children who are not their own. There are support groups for grandparents raising grandchildren and they welcome those who do not exactly fit that description. As with other extenuating circumstances, it is imperative that we seek assistance in dealing with the unique complexities of our situation.

The AD/HD Child and Siblings

Sibling rivalry creates strain and frustration in every family. In families where there are children with AD/HD, the issue of sibling rivalry can be greatly exaggerated. These siblings' perceptions are miles apart. Each perceives the other as the antagonist, and each feels completely justified in his response to the malicious actions of the other. This is the case in our family. Neither child is willing to recognize and acknowledge participation in the conflict. Apologies are rarely heartfelt. Compromises are made only when forced upon them by an adult. Each feels that the other receives more attention and favoritism. Opinions are expressed as fact, and each child is willing to fight to prove that he or she is right and the other wrong. To disagree politely is completely foreign for them. Each feels that it is his or her responsibility to monitor and correct the other and to alert the adults of any infractions. I sometimes feel as though I should wear a whistle and referee uniform. They sometimes try to conspire with one another against me, but they cannot usually remain united long enough to pull it off.

My youngest child, Brandi, does not have AD/HD. This is a blessing for which I am most appreciative. She does, however, have two role models with AD/HD. This is a definite disadvantage. She is not yet old enough to understand that the other two have a biological disadvantage and I am not inclined to tolerate similar behaviors from her. Between Brandi and either of her siblings, there is a better chance of amicability than between the two with AD/HD. She is more willing to be flexible and to avoid conflict than the other two.

Many challenges arise with non-AD/HD children as a result of parents spending an extensive amount of energy on the child with AD/HD. It is hard for the non-AD/HD child to understand why her siblings' behavior seems to be tolerated. It is also easy for her to resent the child with AD/HD.

In a family with openness and honesty, children welcome the information necessary to understand the dynamics of the family unit. Children are inherently compassionate beings. It is important to establish parameters within the family structure that honor the spirit of each family member. It is also important to provide siblings without AD/HD an opportunity to experience our focused attention. This can be very difficult to do, but it is essential.

I find scheduled family meetings to be very helpful. The children all know that on Sunday evening, before the family movie, we will have a meeting. We will review the previous week and discuss upcoming events. This is an opportunity for them to bring up any issues that are of concern to them. They know that it is a safe time to share feelings and requests. It is also an opportunity for goal-setting and new relationship commitments.

These meetings are relatively simple to facilitate. Ground rules should be reviewed prior to each meeting. A climate of compassion and empathy must be established to ensure each person's confidence in the process. One person speaks at a time; a talking stick can be used as a visual reminder of whose turn it is to speak. The person speaking must use "I" statements. For example, it is better to say, "When Nick won't share his Game Boy with me, I feel..." instead of "Nick is so rude to me..." Those who are responding must also respond with "I" statements. Anytime there is a conflict presented, it is important to facilitate a compromise so that everyone leaves the meeting feeling as though something was accomplished on their behalf. Prior to ending the meeting, always ask each person what they need and make sure each person's needs are met in some way. If someone is unhappy and the meeting must end, it is important to continue working together until they feel better. Never send anyone away from the meeting feeling bad about what has transpired!

Family Outings and Vacations

We cannot hide away in our homes with these children to avoid observable chaos and public humiliation. We have to venture out into the world in search of fun and worldly experiences. It is important that our children have opportunities to develop and practice their public appearance skills. It is also important that we not deny them typical childhood experiences such as family outings and vacations.

Some of the most stressful events in my life have been family outings and vacations. Because our children are so unpredictable, difficult to manage, and inept in unfamiliar surroundings, the family outing can go sour in a hundred different ways. Regardless of how you choose to travel, there is no McDonald's Playland in the car, on the bus, on the train, or on the plane. The children must be confined in a relatively small area in order to get from point A to point B. Confining a child with AD/HD to a small area is not usually a good idea, especially not a small area with a lot of other people.

A simple camping trip can become a nightmare. Our family and another went on such a nightmarish adventure one year in the San Juan Mountains. Within a matter of minutes, the children had disappeared. They had climbed up the steepest cliff imaginable and were found walking along a six-inch-wide ledge. When questioned about their adventure, they explained that they had been talking about God and thought if they climbed the mountain, like Moses, God might talk to them. Clearly, this was an impulsive excursion.

When Heather was two and three, we literally had to put her on a long leash and tie one end to a tree to keep her nearby. Later, when she was too old to tie to a tree, she became lost on every camping trip prior to the age of eight. She disappeared in the blink of an eye.

Road trips are difficult with three children jumping and screaming in the back. Finally, Nickolas is old enough for a Game Boy. Any parent of an AD/HD child understands how completely engaged an "innattentive" child can suddenly become when given some type of video game to play with. The problem now is the fighting with his sister over the Game Boy. The kids are too active to be in a car for a long road trip, but we forge onward nevertheless. Just getting there is incredibly stressful. By the time we arrive at our destination, my nerves are frayed and I have no tolerance for fun of any kind. I am exhausted, but somehow, our children are ready to run.

Keeping track of our children at such exciting places as Disneyland is a harrowing task. Waiting in line is not pleasant with an AD/HD child. The excitement makes them cranky and over-stimulated. When you get home, you swear you will never go on another vacation. The funny thing is that by next year, our memories have faded somewhat and we do not remember it being so bad—so we do it again.

Why do we do it? We do it for the same reasons other families do it. We do it for the memories and for those golden moments when we are able to see the exquisite joy in our children's eyes. I have photos of Heather dancing with the Disneyland characters in "The Hunchback of Notre Dame Parade" and of my children with Mickey Mouse and Goofy. Most importantly, I have photos of my children smiling and loving life at Disneyland. Years later, as we look at those pictures, we remember only the good things about that trip and the aggravations are just an amusing afterthought.

I load my kids up once or twice a year and go to Texas to visit my family. This does not seem so bad. Perhaps by now we have made a routine out of it. The first 100 miles of the trip require a stern hand and then the kids do okay. It is a fairly predictable journey because we have done it many times before. They are especially good on the way to Aunt Doris and Uncle Buddy's house because they get to swim in the pool when we get there. The trip home is the hardest. It seems as though there is nothing to look forward to.

I have to be honest and say that I have not ventured on a plane trip with all of my children. Quite frankly, I am afraid to. I am afraid that they would be the loudest kids on the plane. The airline would have to reserve one restroom for our family alone. We would have to take so much stuff to keep them entertained that it would never fit in the carry-on bin. I am also afraid that if we had a layover or even a simple change of planes, I would never make it to the next plane with all of my children. I am afraid they would open the emergency exit, or set off the smoke alarm in the restroom. There are just too many opportunities for disaster on a plane.

I am sure I would never do a bus ride. I would not want to be that close to my children for that much time. They could never be that close to each other! We would never make it out of town.

I did take a trip on Amtrack when Nickolas and Heather were very young. As I recall, it was a challenge. We went to see my dad—from Albuquerque to Oregon. It was a very long ride (two days and two nights, as I recall), and somehow, they managed not to sleep at all. I will never do it again.

I have learned that regardless of where we are going and how we are getting there, I have to plan, plan, plan for them to have things to do. Because they need to change activities often to remain interested, we must have crayons and coloring books, story books and picture books, pillows and blankets, teddy bears and baby dolls, pocket games and Game Boy. We must stop often and change the seating arrangements. We must have children's music to play and extra clothes. It helps to have healthy snacks (fruit, crackers, carrots, etc.), drinks, and extra money.

Family Games

I like to play games. I grew up with a deck of cards in my hands and the weekly games I'd play at my grandparents' house taught me a great deal about life. I learned that you really can have fun even if you don't win. I learned that you have to work hard to win because my grandmother never gave a game away. And I learned the most precious moments in life are those spent enjoying the company of those you love.

I really looked forward to passing on my love of a good game to my children. I never knew family games would bring so much mayhem! Game playing is not a typical strength for an AD/HD child. There's the whining and the crying about drawing a bad card or domino. Then there's the boasting and advice giving by the player who is experiencing an obvious run of good luck. Turn taking is definitely a challenge; no one can remember whose turn it is even though we always go counterclockwise. We have an "options announcer" to point out all the possibilities that can be seen for the person whose turn it is. Offensive comments and hurt feelings are common. Of course, we always begin a game by making a "deal." The deal is that no one will cry or whine, give advice, point out the options of others, make offensive comments, or be hurt by the offensive comments of others. The deal is usually disregarded immediately.

My job is to keep track of whose turn it is and give gentle reminders, monitor all comments, console those hurt by offensive comments, point out advice giving and option announcing, make sure the rules of the game are followed, and see that no one gets hurt! Needless to say, by the end of the game my nerves are a bit frayed. On a good game night, no one goes to bed angry.

There is value in the mayhem, however. Amid all the craziness, there is laughter. We do joke around and enjoy our time together. It also gives my children an opportunity to practice game playing at home and to learn the same lessons I learned from the experience in my youth. Hopefully, the skills they develop at home will carry into social game-playing scenarios and, more importantly, into their adult lives.

Daily Life

It may be true that our families have more excitement than most. It is also true that we will have some good stories to tell our grandchildren. It is too easy to get caught up in the challenge of it all and miss the golden opportunities and the moments of exquisite delight.

We can choose to fight against our challenging lives or we can rise above it all and learn not to sweat the small stuff. We can be embarrassed by our children, or we can learn to laugh at our embarrassment. We make the difference.

I think my house is messier than many others. I am positive my kids are louder. I am pretty sure I attend more meetings at the school than my neighbors do. My neighbors may think I do not supervise my children since they often see me searching for them. I repeat myself a lot more than other parents probably do. Homework is a struggle at our house. We have a more difficult time with bedtime, bathtime, wake-up time, dinnertime, and playtime than other families. More or less, though, we are like other families. We live together, play together, laugh together, fight together, and we love one another.

With intervention, education, and compassion, most days can be good days. When we learn not to live in crisis, the challenges that arise are manageable. Day to day is not so bad when we accept our children for who they are and when we make a commitment to being the best parents we can be. When we decide upon a path of intervention that is right for our child and our family, what once seemed overwhelming will seem manageable. When we learn to honor the spirit within our child, we see more and more the magical being that we are so privileged to share our time with. When we take care of ourselves, we are better able to take care of our children. When we take care of our marriage, we are better equipped to raise our children.

Knowing that life is a process, it should come as no big surprise that raising a child with AD/HD is also a process. We can relax and learn to enjoy it.

Affirmation: I acknowledge the unique qualities of my family life. Knowing that God expresses in an infinite variety of ways, I also know that God expresses within this blessed family. I accept the uniqueness of my family and give thanks for our individuality. I know that this home and this family are blessed with the presence of God in every moment. Our home is filled with love and peace. Our family shares in the spirit of harmony and joy. I accept for myself patience and wisdom. Everything is in divine perfect order, unfolding perfectly and beautifully.

5

Discipline

Discipline is a pressing issue for parents and teachers of AD/HD children. These children need more discipline than others because of the disorder. A parent begins to feel that her only job in life is to discipline her child. Teachers feel as though the discipline issues in the classroom prevent them from teaching.

How to discipline is a question with as many answers as there are seekers. We are not sure, as a society, what the best approach to disciplining children might be. Those of us who have children with AD/HD have an even more difficult time determining how we should discipline our children.

So much of the answer lies in the particular needs of our child in combination with our own philosophy and personality. There are no hard-and-fast answers to the issue of discipline. There are, however, some basic guidelines that can be helpful.

The most difficult obstacle to effective discipline is our own anger. When you have told a child over and over again not to leave the yard without permission and he continues to cause you to search the neighborhood for him, it is natural to become angry. When you have asked a child sixteen times to take her shoes to her bedroom and the shoes are still in the middle of the floor, it is natural to become angry. It is natural, but it is not productive. My children respond to my anger and not to the issue. I may yell that I am sick and tired of the shoes in the middle of the floor (I may even throw in a few other things I'm sick and tired of) and how I have told her sixteen times to pick them up. She will then pick up the shoes. Her mental and emotional response is one of irritation with me for becoming angry. She thinks that I have lost it. Her focus is on my emotional breakdown or the insult of my response instead of her own behavior.

What purpose does anger serve in raising and teaching children with AD/HD? It is important that our children experience the reality that their actions can and do make people angry. Other than that, I am not sure that anger has any place in an interaction between myself and a child. Ideally, I could state the fact that I was angry and walk away until my anger was resolved.

My emotional responses are always about me and not about my child. I cannot pretend that my children are somehow responsible for my anger, my sadness, my depression, or my frustration. When I am reacting with these emotions, I am not centered. I have not arrived at a place within myself where I can deal effectively with my child. Only I have command of this. I am the one who must remedy the situation.

If you find yourself reacting out of emotion, I suggest that you distance yourself for a period of time until you can see what must be done. The timeless recommendation to walk away and count to ten is still good advice. I have to get away from the situation that is causing my frustration, then look at where I am and what I need to do to avoid the frustration. I must take action for myself. Once I do these things, I usually see an improvement in my children's behavior. This confirms for me that it really was my stuff.

We tend to be attached to outcomes. This is true for most aspects of our life and it is especially true as it relates to our children, both at home and in the classroom. These attachments lead to emotional responses and reactions. We must be willing to provide guidance, direction, and consequences for our children and still be able to release our attachments to the choices they will make.

When we are centered in peace and harmony, we are able to effectively discipline our children. How can we discipline an exceptional child if we have not first learned to discipline ourselves? The first step to effective discipline is to be free from emotional distress.

I make a clear distinction between discipline and punishment. Punishment is the act of imposing a negative stimulus after a behavior we do not want repeated. Research has shown there is little value in punishment. For an AD/HD child especially, a punishment does not necessarily decrease the unwanted behavior. Punishment does not typically have a meaningful connection to the act being punished. Discipline is teaching a child how to behave acceptably and to be accountable for her own actions. It is more consistent with molding and shaping as opposed to bending and breaking. Discipline includes consequences, both negative and positive, for certain behaviors. Furthermore, the consequences are directly tied to the behavior being shaped. For example, a child who stays out twenty minutes past his curfew might have twenty to forty minutes taken off his next outing.

What Our Children Need

Structure and Routine

Children with AD/HD need structure and routine more than other children. Predictability equals stability in their lives. It also provides them with a greater opportunity to experience success when they are presented with a situation they have encountered before.

At home, they need to know what their chores are each day. It is best if there is little to no variance in their responsibilities. In this way, they are given an extended amount of time to become responsible for their particular jobs and to develop a habit of doing those things daily. Simple things such as brushing their teeth and putting dirty clothes in the hamper can seem like enormous obstacles to a parent when, day after day, their child is unable to remember these things without several reminders. By insisting on a routine, a habit of doing the things we want them to do will develop. Without consistent structure, however, this process will take much longer.

Our kids also need structure because they tend to be negotiators. If bedtime varies each evening, they automatically think that it is an issue open to debate. Each evening, they will attempt to negotiate a bedtime that suits their immediate needs and desires. If bedtime is 8:30 P.M. every evening, without fail, they will eventually learn that it is not an issue of controversy.

These negotiations begin before we even know our child has AD/HD. They begin when she first asks for a cookie. You give her one. She looks up at you and says, "Two?" This is where the career negotiation begins and it does not ever end. We issue a command, then the next words out of his mouth are, "How about . . . ?" Something inside of these kids tells them that everything is negotiable. The key is in knowing that *every time you negotiate with your child, you are reinforcing that belief.*

We have two choices here. We can either take a hard-line stance and teach our kids that what we say is not negotiable. Or we can try to teach our children to hear us when we say that a particular issue is not negotiable. "Because I said so" is a valid explanation. I used to think that my children deserved a response to their queries about why I had chosen to do things a certain way. What I eventually figured out is that never once did they respond to my explanation with, "Oh, now I understand, thank you kindly for the explanation and I will not bother you about this anymore." I was always met with more questions and a better persuasive oration on why I would be wise to change my position. My advice now is to tell it like it is. Listen to your kids. Change if you are wrong, but hold your ground if you are not. My explanation now is, "You have my answer." No matter what they continue to say, I can continue to repeat, "You have my answer." Eventually, they go away.

Janet worked with Roger for ten years trying to develop the routine of picking up his toys when he was finished playing with them. Time and time again, Roger would move on to another activity, leaving the remnants of his previous activity strewn about the house. Time and time again, Janet would interrupt Roger from his newest passion to have him clean up the mess he left. This was much to his dismay, of course, and no fun for Janet. One summer day, Janet observed the strangest thing. Without prompting, and without beginning something new, Roger put away the toys he had just finished playing with. What an amazing sight! At eleven years of age, Roger was cleaning up his mess entirely on his own initiative! Since that momentous occasion, there have been other times when Roger has done this, though he still requires reminders much of the time. Because Janet worked diligently to create and enforce this routine, she is now able to see that it is, in fact, working. She continues to provide the necessary structure to ensure that Roger continues to develop the ability to follow a routine.

Predictability and Consistency

At school, our children will perform better with consistency. If they are to put completed assignments in a basket on the teacher's desk every time, they will learn to do so. It is important to note that this simple act is not necessarily simple for an AD/HD student. If the teacher varies the place or the manner in which assignments are to be turned in, the student is likely to become frustrated and perhaps confused.

Our children need predictability and consistency. Often when things are not going well with my children, I can see that I have not felt predictable and consistent. When I place my children in unfamiliar situations with little or no predictability and consistency, the stage is set for frustration for them and myself.

One summer, I had a terrible time with day-care arrangements and I was carting my kids around with me most of the time. At the time, we owned our own landscaping business, and the responsibilities that went with that dictated that occasionally I drop everything to tend to business matters. My kids do not respond well to this at all. Any kid would do poorly in this situation, but for a child with AD/HD, it's a recipe for disaster. Each day was different, so there was no way for them to predict what might happen. As a result, every characteristic of AD/HD was exaggerated and we barely survived the summer.

Prepare for Change

Change is an inevitable part of life. Most adults are resistant to change. Even change for the best can send us reeling into confusion and frustration. This is even truer for our children. They have to practice a response over and over to get it right. In the face of change, they immediately become overstimulated and are unable to slow the processes in the brain that would reason them through the situation, find a similar situation in memory, and make a good choice about how to respond. This is why, when we take our children to do something wonderful and new, we end up regretting the gesture and wondering why our child cannot appreciate our efforts and behave accordingly.

By preparing our children for change, we can drastically reduce the likelihood of a negative reaction. We need to give them advance notice of the change and solicit their responses to it. Even if it is a desired change, we must discuss with them all the possibilities they may encounter in the new situation and how they can respond. Have a plan. Introduce the change in advance. Having discussed the upcoming change, if the child has a difficult time in the new situation, you have a plan of which to remind him.

Judy is very familiar with the need to prepare her AD/HD daughter Rachael for any change, no matter how slight. Whenever they go to the store, for example, Judy prepares four-year-old Rachael for what is about to happen. She explains to her that they are going into a place of business and they talk about that store. Judy tells her what the expectations are while in this place. Rachael must stay with her and she must not touch anything. The dialogue prepares Rachael for the new environment. It also cues her in to the fact that there is a change in expectation from this moment to the moment coming up. It prepares her for the change.

Judy has also become aware that she must prepare Rachael again if they leave the first store and go directly to another store. Because our children tend not to generalize, they most likely will not go into the second store understanding that the same rules and expectations apply. If they leave Radio Shack and then go to Wal-Mart, Judy will prepare Rachael by reminding her of all the things she likes at Wal-Mart, telling her what they are there to accomplish, and explaining the expectations while at Wal-Mart. If Judy does not prepare Rachael, the experience is usually one of chaos and frustration.

Visual Aids

AD/HD kids need more visual aids—notes, reminders, and charts—than other kids do. A daily "To Do" list can save you, the parent, from having to repeat each item on the list daily. However, you will have to refer your child to the list time and time again. You will also have to check the list with them for items they missed.

When having our children perform a new or seldom-required task, a note is helpful. Written instructions can save a lot of redirection time. When preparing for a camping trip, for example, it is a good idea to make a list for your child of things he can do to help prepare for the trip. If your child cannot remember to lock the door on his way out, a written note on the front door may do the trick. However, you cannot leave the same note two days in a row because he will not see it the second day; a bigger note or a different-colored note will be necessary.

Younger children with AD/HD seem to respond well to charts. For nonreaders, illustrated charts can be bought or made. A daily chart with tasks or behaviors listed or depicted in which the child earns stars or stickers is an incentive to most young children. As they get older, the stars and stickers are not enough in and of themselves, so cashing them in for prizes becomes a better incentive. Prizes do not necessarily have to be material; computer time, a family movie, time alone with Mom or Dad, a friend to sleep over, or a trip to Grandma's house are all great prizes to reward the efforts of a child.

Reminders

The AD/HD child needs more verbal reminders than most other kids. "I get so tired of repeating myself" is a common cry for the parent of an AD/HD child. We must learn to repeat ourselves without emotion. Our children will have to be told over and over again. It is the nature of this disorder and it is one of the things we must accept. It is important to make sure that you have the child's attention before you speak with her. Once you have given her something to do, ask her to repeat it to you. Once she has done this, send her on her way. When you see her distracted, ask her what it is she needs to do. If she has forgotten, remind her of your instructions. This is one of the most common situations in which we lose patience with our children, and become demeaning or angry when they forget or become distracted. We must remember that our frustration is our own. A gentle reminder may be, "Please remember that I asked you to put the clean clothes from the washer into the dryer and turn on the dryer. I would really like it if you would do this right away." This will probably yield better results than a tirade about how you have already said it fourteen times. It will most likely work better than threats also.

It is John's job to get the children off to school in the mornings. He had a hard time with reminders initially, but has learned the importance of providing reminders to his AD/HD daughter. He would like it if Sarah would get dressed without supervision and be ready for breakfast when he is, but he has learned that Sarah is not there yet. She still requires reminders all along the way, and John has developed a system for providing them. He wakes Sarah up and makes sure she is out of bed before he leaves the room. After he gets the coffee pot going and the water boiling for oatmeal, he checks on Sarah and gently reminds her that she has only twenty minutes to get dressed and he makes sure that she has her clothes picked out before he leaves again. Once the oatmeal is ready, he returns to Sarah's room once again and provides another gentle reminder that she needs to finish getting dressed. This time, he does not leave her in her room; he makes sure she gets to the table to eat. He continues to remind her through breakfast and beyond until she is out the door each morning. John estimates that it takes an average of twenty reminders to get Sarah off to school each day. Once he got over his resistance to this process, he was able to build the reminders into his own morning routine. The end result is that Sarah gets off to school each day dressed, fed, and groomed.

Explanations

Our children need more in-depth explanations and directions about completing a task. They need more dialogue about the task. They need more supervision and more instruction in completing a task—any task. It is very easy to become frustrated by this and begin to speak to our children in a degrading manner. We must learn that they do not ask this of us in order to torture us. This is what they must have in order to learn.

We thought Nickolas would never learn to sweep the floor. Every time he had to sweep, we had to reintroduce the task of sweeping. We had to keep a watchful eye and remind him throughout the task how to do it. It seemed like such a simple task and he seemed to make it so difficult. It was easy to lose sight of the goal, which was to teach Nickolas to sweep the floor. Whatever becomes necessary to meet the goal is what we must do.

The challenge is in delivering the goods without diminishing the child. Is he somehow less of a being because the art of sweeping does not come easily to him? No. So why, then, is it so frustrating for his parents? When we look at it in this light, it is easy to see once again that it is not about the child at all. It is about the adult. Our children, for whatever reason, need additional instructions and explanations. For whatever reason, our child needs for us to go over it again. What our child needs, above all else, is for the adults in his life to be kind and to provide him with what he needs without sending a message that he is not okay because of what he needs.

Our children need to have the task explained in chunks. When we issue a series of instructions, they tend to hear only one of the things we are telling them to do. For example, if you tell an AD/HD child to turn in his homework and get a book for reading, he will get a book for reading, but not turn in his homework. We have to explain and instruct in chunks in order for them to be successful.

Follow-through

Our children will test the waters over and over again to see if things are still the same. They will persevere in their attempts to push the envelope. They will try to see if this time they can sneak a few more minutes of TV time or delay getting their homework done for a little longer. This is why it is so important for us to establish clear guidelines. We must think about what we say before we say it, mean what we say, stand by what we say, and enforce consequences. This is perhaps the most important thing to be said about discipline as it applies to an AD/HD child.

You may notice that the child with AD/HD seems to have an immunity to rules and orders. It does not matter how many times they hear the rules; they know the rules. It does not matter how many times you repeat a command; they know what it is that you have asked them to do. What is so unique is that they perceive the rules to be established as friendly reminders, which can be disregarded at their discretion. No AD/HD child has ever admitted this to me, but I know it to be true! When I give a direct order to my AD/HD child, she will create the appearance that she is going to do what I have told her to do, but unless I follow through with her until the end, she will not actually do it. This is why follow-through is everything. If an AD/HD child knows that they have at least a 50 percent chance that you will not follow through and make sure that they have done what they were told, they figure those are good odds to work with. They need to know that the odds are much closer to 100 percent that you will follow through.

Sharon learned the importance of follow-through when Logan was in the second grade. Logan could not seem to get his monthly field trip permission forms home for her signature prior to the field trip. For the first two field trips of the year, Sharon had to rush over to the school to sign the permission slip so that Logan would be able to go. The second time caused her a great deal of difficulty at work, so she had to find a way to impress upon Logan the importance of getting those permission slips home to be signed. She told Logan that the next time he did not get the permission slip signed and returned to his teacher, she would not come to school to sign the form and he would not be allowed to go on the trip. He was very unhappy with this accountability concept. However, when the next field trip was announced, he managed to get the slip signed and returned. Sharon was relieved. The next field trip, though, Logan did not have the slip signed and returned on time. Logan and Sharon both knew of their arrangement, but Sharon was heartbroken hearing Logan's sobs over the phone. She could not bear to have him miss the field trip, so she drove to the school and signed the form.

Logan didn't bring home permission slips for the next two field trips. Because Sharon had not followed through, they were essentially back to square one. Finally, she had to follow through with the consequence she had given Logan months before. She stood her ground and Logan spent the day in another classroom. Logan never forgot his permission slip again. Once he understood that the consequence would be enforced, he managed to get the job done.

Patience

Our children are likely to take forever to complete a task. Have you ever sent your child into his room to clean it and feared you would never see him again? Have you ever wondered how it can take two hours to take out the trash? Do you ever wonder why? You are not alone. The child with AD/HD is very slow to complete a task. The best way to combat this is with incentives. On housecleaning day, you may offer an hour at the pool if everything is done by 2:00 P.M. Most of us feel that the best way to get through something we do not want to do is to do it quickly. AD/HD children do not subscribe to this theory. It is as if they somehow think that if they take a really long time to do it, they will not ever have to do it again. The reason they take a long time is because they are excessively distracted, both externally and internally. I sometimes think my child has become so distracted by the thought of not wanting to do something, that he is immobilized.

They are likely to whine and complain and cry and even become completely distraught and overwhelmed by a simple request. It is amazing to watch. You ask your child to please clear the dinner dishes. You had pizza and you used paper plates. They collapse on the floor crying. You think they have just had some sort of medical emergency. But no, they are mumbling something. Upon further inspection, you find that they are completely distraught over your request. "Why do I have to do everything? I never get a break. I always have to do this. Now I won't be able to do what I wanted to do. Why doesn't someone

else have to do this? I'm having a terrible day." These are real
tears! The only thing I have found to do is to make an attempt
at consoling my child by saying something like, "I can see that
you are upset. I'm sorry you feel so bad. [Hug] When you are
finished crying, please clear the dishes off the table and then
you may do what you were going to do." Pointing out to the
child that they have now spent twice as much time crying as it
would have taken to do the job is pointless. It will only frustrate
them further. Becoming angry with the child will not help. The
only real option is to let them have their moment.

Our children respond well to novelty. They love it when we
are creative. They love it when we add pizzaz to their life. After
all, they add a lot of pizzaz to our life! If you make something
slightly different each time, without removing the consistency,
they will respond positively. This may seem to be a contradiction
on the surface. They do need consistency, but they also need
novelty. Keeping in mind that they are highly stimulated by what
is new, interesting, and different, our best chance at success is to
create a highly stimulating way of parenting and teaching.

Things That Will Not Work

Common negative responses include yelling, lecturing, spank-
ings, guilt trips, words that hurt our children, and even violence.
All kids push their parents to their limits from time to time. The
AD/HD child has no awareness of the limits; therefore, he
pushes his parents beyond their limits. It is too easy, after a long
day at the office, to lose control with this demanding child.
When we learn to take care of ourselves and honor the spirit
within us, then we will be better able to respond constructively
to our child.

Yelling

Yelling is a common response to being frustrated with a child.
Often we blame the child for our yelling. We remind her that we
did say it nicely five times before we yelled and she could have
avoided our yelling by responding appropriately the fifth time.

The problem here lies in shifting responsibility from ourselves to our child. The AD/HD child has so much to improve upon, the expectation that they can somehow improve upon our responses is simply unfair. The truth of the matter is that we are yelling because we are reacting emotionally to the situation. This is not about the child. Yelling at our children is demeaning. Have you ever noticed the diminished look in their eyes after they have been yelled at? A commitment to honor the spirit within the child is a commitment to be a source of strength and inspiration, a guiding light, not an intimidating voice. When we feel like yelling, the best approach is to make sure the child is safe and walk away until we have released the emotion surrounding the issue.

As the parent or teacher of a child with AD/HD, you cannot afford to lose your cool. If and when you *do* lose your cool and yell at a child, communicate with him about the situation once everyone has calmed down. Talk with him about how you feel when you yell. Then allow the child to talk about how he feels when he is yelled at. Listen with your entire being to how your child feels when he is yelled at. If you really listen in this way, you will empathize with him at the most intimate level. Listening with your heart helps everyone to heal and create better ways of solving problems. Discuss with the child what could have been done differently. This kind of dialogue is invaluable. It is a growth opportunity for each participant. Our children find strength and inspiration in seeing us admit our mistakes and strive for personal improvement. What better modeling could there be?

Lecturing

Many times I have caught myself lecturing to my child. I have to stop and laugh at myself for what I am doing. Most lectures are triggered in the present, but they are about the past and the future. It seems to happen before we are aware of it. We begin with a current issue and then discuss how this has always been a problem and we revisit numerous examples from the past. Then we discuss the serious nature of the problem and how it will impact them in the future. We may even tell stories about people we know or about ourselves. We essentially explain to the child how, if he does not change his ways, his entire future is on the line.

Our experience leads us to anticipate the future and we want to share our insight with our children. But children have no concept of ten years from now, nor do they have any idea what we are talking about when we make reference to "the real world." Most of the time, a child tunes out our lecture. If he does not tune out, he can become either resentful or anxious about the future. This is an undue burden to place on a child. Our focus must be in the present, not the future. Though we see how a behavior not changed can have a long-term detrimental effect, we must ask ourselves if it is really necessary or beneficial to share this with our child. Do we really want our children, who have so much to work on today, to be worried about their success in a thousand tomorrows? The best approach is to deal directly with the current issue as it relates to the present. Our children respond best to what is immediate. The most effective feedback is immediate and concise. If we are worried about our child's future, we must talk to other parents in our situation, to our spouse, or to our friends.

Spanking

Whether or not to spank children has been a heated topic for many years now. When we were children, our parents did not hesitate to spank us. There was no social stigma about spanking a child. That has changed. It is certainly not wise to spank a child in public. It is not my intent to take a position on this controversial issue, but there are some considerations specific to the spanking of an AD/HD child.

There is a lot to be gained from the timeless advice to never spank a child in anger. It is important to closely monitor the response gained from spanking an AD/HD child. Does spanking encourage him to change the behavior, or does it cause him to focus on his misguided perception of the situation?

In some schools, children are being taught to define certain forms of discipline as abuse. In the schools' presentation, many children, certainly those with AD/HD, begin to define spanking as abuse.

A child with AD/HD may be more likely to share information that you do not want shared. To our embarrassment, they may also be more likely to exaggerate that information. On more than one occasion, my children have shared our darkest moments with a captivated audience at school. I was very fortunate to be friends with the counselor at one elementary school my children attended. She would share with me the horrific stories that my children told in group counseling sessions. My children took events from our family and exaggerated them to epic proportions. They shared the horrors of their life with awe-struck children.

At another elementary school, with a counselor who did not know me, my children continued to share their exaggerated stories. One particular incident, involving my daughter, happened recently. She had gotten very angry at home and punched a hole in her bedroom window, leaving a cut on her arm, which began at her palm and ended near her elbow. I mentioned to her that I would not go to school and tell people that I had gotten cut because I punched out my window. The next day at school, she went to the nurse's office for sympathy and ice. When the nurse asked her how she had been cut, she responded, "I'm not allowed to tell you." Fortunately, I arrived at the school about this time to deliver Heather's lunch and was able to clarify the situation. If not, no doubt she would have ended up in the counselor's office.

Guilt Trips

The use of guilt is not new nor is it specific to parents of children with AD/HD. However, it is imperative that we understand that guilt is only productive in small doses. A small dose of guilt is like a vaccine: it can reduce the likelihood of a recurrence of the behavior. Healthy guilt originates from within. Too much guilt leads to shame. Our children already struggle with self-esteem issues. I know there is no parent who intends to rob his child of self-worth. Imposing shame on a child is the most depleting thing we can do. We must be careful not to cause our children to feel shame for having AD/HD. It serves no purpose for them to feel guilty about something they cannot change.

Keep in mind that, given the choice, they would choose not to have AD/HD. We must focus on the learning process. We must focus on helping our children learn to compensate for their differences and reach their greatest potential. We cannot do this with guilt and shame. This is a lengthy process and success can be greatly enhanced with support and encouragement or greatly diminished with guilt and shame.

Words That Hurt

It is easy, in our frustration, to use words that hurt our children. Sometimes these words cut right through to the very soul of a child. Everyone remembers a time in their childhood when an adult said something that hurt them deeply. These words are a direct assault on the spirit of a child. When we say things about who they are or the nature of their being, they cannot help being hurt. A constant barrage of these hurts can convince a child that the words spoken about them are true. If we continuously tell a child she is stupid, incompetent, insensitive, mean, or lazy, she will come to believe it about herself. We must be careful not to implant a self-fulfilling prophecy within our children. They will begin to be that which they have been told they already are. We must be cautious and deliberate with the words we use. We must learn to speak to our children from love and not from frustration.

Violence

Violence is no stranger to many families with an AD/HD child. Violence can erupt between siblings, between parents, and between the parent and the child. It is easy to reach this point. Perhaps those without a child with AD/HD cannot understand how this happens.

Those of us with children who have significant difficulties do understand. We understand the exhaustion, physically and emotionally, that comes with the task of raising a child with special needs. We understand that because our children can be so difficult, we have fewer opportunities to get away and recuperate. We understand that the demands are so intense that sometimes we feel that we are in a pressure cooker and will explode at any given moment.

It is important that we protect ourselves and our children from violence. If we feel there is a danger that we may become violent, we must get help. There are many psychologists and other therapists who specialize in AD/HD issues who can help parents to cope effectively without violence.

The most helpful things for me have been my own spiritual journey and my association with CHADD. These two combined have helped me to keep things in perspective. I have resources I did not have before and I have ways to get away when I need to. Even with the help of a therapist, it is imperative that we have a support network. We must have people to talk with who understand.

Sadly, it is sometimes our children who resort to violence. Any child, with or without AD/HD, who becomes violent is a child in need. We must immediately seek the advice of a trained professional using whatever means necessary to secure help for the child.

When the frustration becomes overwhelming, we must walk away and reenergize ourselves. We must always return to the responsible rearing of our children. We must be their parent, their confidant, and their advocate. We must find within ourselves the strength of character to carry on. I believe that we all want to. I also believe that, with support and with information, we can honor the spirit within our child. In twenty years, as I sit across the dinner table from my grown child, I will feel certain that I have done all I could have done to help him to be happy and whole.

Affirmation: I graciously accept the responsibility of teaching my child. I embrace the opportunity to grow personally as I share in my child's growth experience. I am guided intuitively to provide guidance and direction for my child. In every situation, I am peaceful and calm, able to give from the depths of my soul. When I look into my child's eyes, I see God loving me through him and I honor that spirit within him through every action I take.

6

The Oppositional Defiant Child

All parents will experience the occasional "You can't make me" attitude from their child. This is typically a surprising occurrence followed by a swift and meaningful consequence for such behavior.

The oppositional defiant child is the one whose *prevailing* attitude or disposition opposes and defies virtually everything. Nothing pleases this child. Any satisfaction is short-lived. They are risk takers beyond that of the ordinary AD/HD child. They seem to have an automatic device within them that says *"No!"* and creates havoc in any and every situation. They will throw the loudest fits, the most often, in as many public places as possible. These are the children who can reduce their parents to tears on a daily basis.

It is difficult to instill in them a strong sense of right and wrong. Even if they can verbalize the difference between right and wrong, they are not often inclined to choose rightly. Upon discussing inappropriate behaviors, they seldom seem remorseful or inclined to change the behavior. They tend to shift responsibility or blame from themselves to another party.

It is important to note that this extreme behavior is not characteristic of Attention Deficit/Hyperactivity Disorder. There is something else going on. However, there is a significant percentage of children with AD/HD who are also diagnosed with oppositional defiant disorder.

I have given birth to three children. Immediately following the birth of each child, the doctor wrapped the beautiful bundle of joy in a blanket and gave it to me to cuddle and adore. Two of my babies immediately stopped crying and gazed into my eyes. I talked to them and we were immersed in a beautiful shared moment.

One beautiful bundle of joy responded differently. She did not stop crying. She did not gaze into my eyes nor did she seem to listen to anything I was saying to her. She simply screamed with all her might. After twenty minutes, much to my relief, the nurses took her to the nursery, where she promptly stopped crying and took a long nap. My first moments with Heather were to foreshadow the next seven years of her life.

As an infant, she was inconsolable. She lost her voice at three weeks of age. I was actually grateful to have some quiet. Even though she continued to cry, it was not audible. I would hold her and rock her and walk with her and bounce her, but nothing I did ever worked. She clearly preferred the baby swing to my arms. She cried and cried. I nursed her for a few months, but she was a cranky eater. She did not ever sleep through the night as a baby. (That would not come until age four.) There were some wonderful moments, though they were not as frequent as I would have liked.

The terrible twos began somewhere around her first birthday. When I said "Stop!," her response was to run faster. When I said "No!," her response was to do it more quickly. It seemed that every time I let her out of my sight, there was a price to pay. It did not matter how many times or how many ways I tried to teach her to be safe; she did not get the message. She could not be left alone with other children for fear of what she might do to them. She was thrown out of two preschools for the wounds she inflicted on other children. When the other children took naps, she alone remained awake and active. When the others sat nicely and ate their snack, she tried to take their food from them. On the playground, if all the swings were occupied, that was not to deter her; she would pull the other child off the swing or simply pinch and bite him until he relinquished possession of the swing to her. These types of behaviors continued well into her third year.

By the time she was four, she seemed to be making some improvements, but she was still impossible to manage. Her negative energies became channeled differently. It often seemed as though her life's mission was to drive me to an emotional meltdown. She thought the walls of our home were her drawing board. I once repainted her room because I noticed she was no longer writing on the walls. She showed her appreciation of the clean walls when she took a crayon, and beginning at one side of her door, drew a line across all four walls, and ended at the other side of the door.

I took her to McDonald's Playland one afternoon soon after my younger daughter was born. It was particularly busy that afternoon. As all the children played in the ball cage, I found another mom to visit with. Her son came to her during our conversation and said, "Mom, that little girl in the ball cage is dead." His mother patted him on the head and sent him back to play. When the little boy returned to say that, after closer inspection, he was convinced that the little girl was dead, we decided to check it out. From outside the ball cage, I could see Heather's arm protruding from underneath the mass of yellow, blue, green, and red balls. I called to her repeatedly and got no response. The little boy crawled in and tried to coax her out from under the balls; he, too, got no response. There must have been eight or ten other children in there at the time. I handed my newborn baby to a complete stranger and crawled into the ball cage. When I lifted Heather, she was like a rag doll, absolutely limp. Someone screamed for the manager to call 911. I laid Heather down and lightly tapped her cheeks. I could see that she was breathing normally. I tried to lift her eyelids to look at her pupils, but I was unable to do so. An unconscious person is not able to resist having their eyelids lifted, so I knew that she was not hurt. I said things to her like, "Heather, you have to open your eyes for Mommy. This is not funny. You are making me afraid. All these people want to know that you are okay. Open your eyes, Heather." My adrenaline level was so elevated that I could hardly breathe. My heart was pounding so loudly that everything else sounded muffled. A woman pushed her way through the large crowd that had gathered around my child. I heard the sirens of the ambulance that had been called. The woman said, "Get out of the way, I know CPR." I replied, "She doesn't need CPR, she is fine." I could hear the gasps of the crowd and read their judgments about what kind of horrible mother I must be to respond in such a way. Thankfully, the woman I had visited with must have known I was not crazy. She said, "Heather, would you like an ice cream?" My child sat bolt upright and said, "Sure," with a great big smile. Right about then, the paramedics arrived. They insisted on checking her out; of course, she was fine. The manager brought her an ice cream. It was all I could do to keep from going into hysteria. The adrenaline rush had not gone away once I knew there was no real danger. I put her and the baby into the car and drove home. I put her in her room and told her she was absolutely not to come out under any circumstances. I put the baby to bed. Then I cried for most of the afternoon. When my husband came home and saw me in this condition, he could not understand the profound impact of this experience.

Maybe most children do things like this on occasion, though I doubt it. None of my friends' children have ever done anything like this. This episode was characteristic of a pattern of behavior. In addition to dramatic episodes like this, there was an overall pattern of lying, cheating, stealing, manipulating, refusal to comply, and destruction. Our everyday life was riddled with drama and chaos. There was never a dull moment with Heather. Life at home was difficult at best and I dreaded any situation that required a public appearance.

These dramatic events eventually shifted away from public places as she grew more aware of herself as a public spectacle. Currently, she does much better in public and at school than she does at home. Her outbursts are primarily limited to the home environment. Any public defiance is displayed only when her parents are with her. She has a very forked tongue, difficulty accepting authority at home, and she experiences a great deal of frustration in many situations.

Heather was diagnosed with oppositional defiant disorder (ODD) at age four. This is the real name of a real disorder with criteria for diagnosis in the *DSM*. The criteria established in the *DSM-IV* is as follows:

- A pattern of negativistic, hostile, and defiant behavior lasting at least six months, with four or more of the following behaviors:
  1. often loses temper
  2. often argues with adults
  3. often actively denies or refuses to comply with adults' requests or rules
  4. often deliberately annoys people
  5. often blames others for his or her mistakes or misbehaviors
  6. is often touchy and easily annoyed by others
  7. is often angry and resentful
  8. is often spiteful or vindictive
- These behaviors create a significant impairment in social, academic, or occupational functioning.
- The behaviors do not occur during the course of a psychotic or mood disorder.
- Criteria is not met for conduct disorder and, for persons over 18, criteria is not met for antisocial personality disorder.

If your child appears to meet this criteria, you may find solace in knowing that there is a name for what you are experiencing. You may find support in your community, in addition to CHADD, for parents of behaviorally challenged children. Your physician will have some treatment options. Psychological services, or counseling, will most likely be a necessity. The greatest cause for concern with an ODD child is the possibility of its progression into a conduct disorder. No parent wants to experience this progression. Therefore, it is imperative that we be proactive, continue to address the changing needs of our child, and be willing to invest in treatment options such as therapy and/or anger management.

As the parent of an ODD child, we face many additional challenges to those encountered by the parent of an AD/HD child. Whereas most schools do not want to place an AD/HD child in a special classroom, they may want to remove the ODD student from the general classroom setting in favor of a classroom for behaviorally and/or emotionally disturbed students. This presents a parent with many things to consider, such as whether or not such a placement is reasonable and appropriate for their child and whether or not such a placement will benefit the child. Every issue discussed in this book is magnified for the parent of an AD/HD-ODD child.

Everything I have presented in regard to an AD/HD child is still pertinent to raising a child with ODD. The oppositional and defiant behaviors can be dramatically improved over time. By honoring the spirit of the oppositional child, you can greatly reduce the need the child has to be oppositional and help her to become more of her "beautiful self."

Heather has improved with age. She has responded well to school and continues to grow and improve. We keep her active with summertime activities, such as the swim team. We make sure that she has something in her life to channel a lot of energy into. She has to be reminded often that I am the parent and she is the child. She becomes visibly upset with me on a daily basis. She scrunches her face into a million distorted signs of her frustration. She flails her arms around wildly as she loudly explains how unreasonable I am. I remind her often of the tone of voice she may use. I remind her of how disrespectful the look on her face is. Regardless of the issues we still face, she is now manageable.

When I am able to shift my thinking about Heather and my approach with Heather, Heather continues to improve. When I am aware that this child was sent to me because I have that special something inside me that she needs, it immediately becomes easier to work with her. That "special something" that I forget I have comes forward to be present.

By honoring the spirit of this child, I have been able to reach her at a deeper level of her being. Instead of working with her at a surface level, I work with her at a spiritual level. That has made all the difference. By honoring her spirit, the spirit within her automatically responds. In spirit, there is always reciprocation. When we love, love is returned to us. The same is true in raising our children. When we honor spirit, spirit honors us.

It is infinitely more challenging to use this approach with a child like Heather. It is even more difficult, however, to make headway using any other approach. Each day we are presented with many challenging moments that increase the demand for us to remain centered while at the same time decreasing our constitution. It is vitally important that we take care of ourselves by nurturing our own spirit so that we can rise to the challenge of helping our child. The rewards are immeasurable. The greatest sense of fulfillment comes from being wholly present for the healing of your child's soul.

As you read through the pages of this book, keep in mind, if you have a child like Heather, that everything applies in multiples. If we have to be consistent with an AD/HD child, we must be *more* consistent with an ODD child. If it is important to honor the spirit of the AD/HD child, it is *more* important that we honor the spirit of the ODD child.

7

Taking Care of You

Many people react to a diagnosis of Attention Deficit/Hyperactivity Disorder with terror and denial while others respond with a sense of relief that there is, in fact, a term to describe their difficulties. Regardless of the initial response to the diagnosis, I think most parents experience the process of grief in all its stages. Grief consists of phases of denial, anger, bargaining, depression, and acceptance. We mourn the expectations that we cannot afford to hold on to. We are angry; our anger takes many forms and is channeled in various directions. Sometimes this anger is with the child. Sometimes this anger is with life or God. I certainly shed a lot of angry tears asking "Why me?" We have a good day and begin to think that this whole diagnosis is bogus. "It was just a phase. She's coming out of it now. We don't need these meds or this doctor or this support group. Everything is normal here."

It is important that we allow ourselves to indulge in our private thoughts and feelings in order to reconcile them. If we do not do this, we cannot help our child. Denying our most horrible thoughts and feelings, or berating ourselves for them, denies us the opportunity to break free of them. When we do not allow ourselves to be depressed or to be angry, the happy face that we plaster on will not sustain us through the next incident or the next wave of emotion.

Like every other parent, we held expectations in our heart for the child we would have. We must grieve the loss of those expectations. We must look squarely at them, acknowledge them, and mourn for the child we thought we would have. I acknowledge that I dreamed my child would be a social butterfly with many friends and the adoration of teachers. This is not the child I have. I grieve for the loss of that dream, that expectation. Then I can accept the truth about the child I do have and embrace him for the beautiful being that he is. Our expectations get in the way of our acceptance.

The very thought of this kind of grieving sends pains of guilt through a parent. We think we are selfish. We are afraid that the grief somehow is a testament to our own inadequacies. We fear experiencing the depth of our own pain.

I remember a horrible time when my daughter was three or four years old. We were having a particularly difficult time with her. She had not yet begun to sleep through the night, so she was up at all hours being mischievous. She did the most bizarre things in public, certainly with the intent to destroy my self-image. She was completely unmanageable. I was a full-time student and my husband was working very hard to get his business off the ground. My husband also did not see the same problems that I saw with our daughter. He somehow did not understand how I could have so much trouble with this sweet child. I was exhausted and depleted. On a visit to my mom's, I sobbed for hours. I vented with her all of my horrible feelings of guilt, anger, resentment, pity, and the like. Fortunately, my mom has always been very supportive and has never criticized my parenting. She held me and validated me and allowed me to be consumed by those feelings. When the storm passed, I was renewed and somehow stronger. I was cleansed. I no longer had to hide from the feelings; they were out in the open for me to acknowledge. I survived this episode, and I was much stronger for it. I have not ever spoken or written the things that I expressed that day, but I assure you that your own thoughts and feelings could be no uglier. There have been many frustrating times with my daughter since then, but I have not since had to experience such a radical purging. I hope that if I do need to experience it again, I will face it with courage and be better off for allowing myself to express my deepest emotions in a way that promotes healing.

It is important that we allow ourselves to indulge in our private thoughts and feelings in order to reconcile them. I recommend that you do this kind of deep purging with someone who is without judgment. To receive a sermon, a lecture, or advice will do you no good and will probably send you reeling into deeper depression. If we do not do this for ourselves, we cannot help our child.

Once we get through this process of grieving, or even while we are still in the midst of it, we can begin to celebrate the child that *is*. This book is about honoring our children for who they are. How boring the world would be without them. How cheated we would be not to have them. To truly honor the spirit of the child with AD/HD, I propose the following steps: acceptance, growth and discovery, practice, patience, and consciousness.

Acceptance

We must accept our child for who he is. Make a list of all the characteristics of your child. Do not label them good or bad, acceptable or unacceptable. Instead, define each characteristic in positive terms. (For example, a child who bombards you with 5,000 questions a day is "curious" or "inquisitive.") Create a mental picture of who he is. Know that your child is uniquely special. Acknowledge that your child has a unique contribution to make in life. Without any desire to change any part of him, embrace him as the gift to you that he is; know that he is a unique gift to the world. Nothing else compares in importance to your complete awareness and unconditional acceptance of your child.

Then it is time to look at your challenges as this child's parent. Again, write them down. What feels challenging about raising this child? Where is your frustration? When writing this down, try not to write statements that are about the child, but about you. (For example, I am bothered by his fidgeting.) Accept that your challenges as a parent are what they are. Do not ask why.

I spent the first three to four years of my daughter's life

asking why and how questions: Why is she the way she is? Why did this happen to me? Why does it have to be this way? How can I change her? How can I make her normal? How will I ever survive this experience? How will she survive? What I finally came to realize was that these questions were not getting me anywhere. There were no answers to these questions.

I began asking different questions: What can *I* do today to be a beneficial presence to my child and my family? What can I do to keep my sanity? What can I believe about this child that will help me to see her differently? These are questions I could find answers for. I realized I had a long road to travel and I could not justify being miserable for twenty years. It is what it is. So, how can I make it beautiful?

In my own process of acceptance, I had this realization about my daughter, Heather:

> She was born with a scream and a holler,
> There was much more of that to follow.
> We had many sleepless nights,
> And lots of angry fights.
> I asked what is this lesson that I must learn,
> For its nature I could not discern.
> I live my life with great passion,
> This child's turmoil I could not fashion.
> She'd be sweet for an instant,
> Then she would resist.
> She screamed and she cried,
> She bit and she lied.
> She disappeared quite often,
> Her temper would not soften.
> I thought God wanted me to be strong,
> I never dreamed I could be wrong.
> I thought God wanted me to be firm,
> I never searched for a more loving term.
> I thought I needed to learn tolerance,
> Yet I never looked to see life's dance.
> This little girl came to me not as my teacher,
> She came because I have the love that can reach her.

When I opened my heart and spirit was here,
Suddenly my lesson was so very clear.
It is not to be strong, firm, or tolerant,
My mission here is much more significant,
I am to protect her and show her the way,
I will guide her to spirit and teach her to pray,
I will help her to see all the goodness she is inside,
And all of life's lessons in her I'll confide.
I will allow her to be mistaken,
And never again will her spirit be forsaken.
I am guided by wisdom and divine intuition,
And I know that our love will come to fruition.
I am free at last; I can finally see,
And allow spirit to nurture both her and me.

Growth and Discovery

Most people are not entirely prepared for ordinary parenting experiences; certainly, no one is prepared for the experience of parenting an AD/HD child. We have been presented with a fabulous opportunity to reach beyond our ordinary capacity. We must make a commitment to become extraordinary parents to our extraordinary children. Time is of the essence, for our level of exceptionality must be one step ahead of theirs or we will become exhausted trying to keep up!

My own personal growth process has inspired me to reach out to my community, develop my spirituality, assist my children in developing a sense of spirituality, and write this book. More importantly, it has made me a happier, more complete person. I am secure enough in who I am to know that my parenting is effective and to know that my children are magnificent just the way they are. In order to effectively parent the child with AD/HD, it is imperative that we have emotional strength, determination, and detachment as well as compassion and sensibility.

Perhaps the first step to this process of growth and discovery is educating ourselves about AD/HD. I began to devour books and tapes and articles that could tell me more about the disorder. I needed to understand what was going on with my children. I needed to know what made them behave as they do. I am still reading and learning. The research is ongoing, and new information and theories are published all the time. It is important that we read and keep up with the latest findings, and that we initiate questions and conversations with our children's doctors and other parents.

After consuming an enormous amount of information, I then have to ask myself, "What do I do with all of this?" So, the journey continues. One inquiry leads me to another and I have not run out of questions yet.

Raising a child with AD/HD has a tendency to consume your energy. It is laborious, no matter what age she is. For our own health and sanity, we must find a way to care for ourselves so we have the necessary reserves to nurture our children. For me, it is a daily practice of meditation and study. I am up each morning before the rest of my family so I can have at least an hour and a half to myself. In that time, I enjoy the quiet, have my coffee, read books that enrich my life, meditate, and pray. It took some time to develop this routine, but now I would not give it up. Through this practice, I honor the spirit within *me*. This is a prerequisite to honoring the spirit within my children.

I recommend that parents find a way to honor the spirit within themselves daily, whether it be through meditation, exercise, yoga, tai chi, or a hot bath. Create a ritual of sacred time and space for yourself. I know if I do not develop and maintain a strong sense of connectedness to my true self and to the power that is greater than I am, I am not effective with my children. When I get off-track with my self-nurturing routine (vacation, summertime, company in town), it becomes apparent right away. I forget my purpose and my role with my children. I am short on patience and compassion. My interactions with my children do not occur at a meaningful, spiritual level.

There are multiple benefits to honoring the spirit within myself. My life is enriched beyond my relationship with my children. Every other aspect of my life benefits from my growth. All my relationships are greatly enhanced. This personal growth is beneficial to my entire family, my friends, and people I encounter each day. It is through my sense of self that I am able to guide my children toward their own.

Parenting teaches us so much about ourselves. So often, something inside me will jump up and say or do something that is astonishing. I love it when it is a positive thing, like the day my son shared with me that he had been thrown out of the Junior Golf Program. Something inside me jumped out and said, "You have created this situation and I will not intervene. I will not deny you the opportunity to make things right with your coach. I will expect you to take care of this tomorrow." My son was shocked that I was not going to bail him out or bawl him out and I was quite pleased with my response. This type of experience is evidence of my growth and progression as a parent. My response was immediate but not impulsive. I was inwardly guided to be and do the very thing that was best for Nickolas.

There are times, though, when I do not respond in a productive manner, like the time I found myself ranting and raving at my children on housecleaning day. I had to stop and ask myself what was going on inside me that was causing me to act this way. I realized I had reconnected to childhood feelings of resentment and was behaving like a maniac. This type of experience is an opportunity to identify and rectify patterns that no longer serve me. I was able to identify the root of my emotions (childhood resentments regarding housework), evaluate the usefulness of the emotion (I found none), and let go of the old pattern (it was no longer necessary).

As we become aware of our interactions with our children on a moment-by-moment basis, and when we are open to seeing what is really there, we experience personal growth beyond our expectations. It is often painful to admit to ourselves that we are reacting with irrational thought patterns, beliefs, and feelings. Our first reaction seems to be to protect those old patterns that may once have been useful or necessary and, in so doing, hurt those we love the most. When you are able to honestly look at your issues, you will be able to heal old wounds and be free from them.

This does not mean that I must always confront my parents on issues that I experienced as hurtful years ago. When I know what they are, I can acknowledge how they once hurt me and realize that this issue cannot continue to cause pain in my life unless I let it. Then I can release it and be free of it. If I am unable to release it, I must seek help in doing so from a spiritual counselor or other therapist.

Personal growth is a never-ending process. It is a wonderful process of discovery about myself that leads me to a greater expression of who I am and what I am all about. It is exhilarating to know that in every moment I am able to choose who I want to be. I cannot stress enough the importance of a commitment to personal growth.

Through personal growth, the doors open to magnificent discoveries about who we are, who our children are, and who we are in this parent-child relationship. Our commitment to such discovery clears a pathway for deep insights and realizations.

The discovery process allows us to look at ourselves in a new way. To discover who we are is an awesome undertaking. It requires endurance and desire. The desire to know oneself intimately will lead to many opportunities for discovery. These opportunities are often accompanied by discomfort or pain. It is not always easy to see who we have chosen to be.

Sometimes, painfully, we realize we have become someone we did not want to be. When confronted with such a realization, most of us will pull out our armor of defense and rationalize how and why it is that we are the way we are. Instead, we should take the opportunity to reprogram our subconscious by consciously choosing who we will be. I must let down my defenses because I do not need them in this process of discovering myself. I must look at myself honestly without fear of being discovered by others.

The discovery that we have become something we do not wish to be is a gift. We are able to look at the characteristic and also discover how and why we developed in this way. There is, at the root of it, a valid reason why we evolved in the way we did. It may have developed as a child. Often, we develop unwanted characteristics as a defense mechanism. These served us well and kept us safe in the past. We can release them now because they are no longer needed.

It may not be possible, at first, to get to the root of the issue by yourself. If you find this to be the case, seek the help of a supportive friend, a spiritual counselor, or a therapist. By asking the right questions, another person can often lead us to the answers we seek. Once we discover the patterns we are perpetuating and the reasons we developed those patterns in the first place, we are free to do with them as we please. We can allow them to continue to influence our life or we can replace them with a new belief and behavior.

To replace an old pattern with a new, we must recognize the truth of our being. These are a few universal truths that may be useful:

- We each have a spiritual connection to the universe in which we live.
- We each have a need to feel this connection to the world around us.
- We each have a desire to be known and understood by others.
- We each have an inherent need to experience great love.

These universal truths can be used as the first step to replacing an old pattern. Acknowledge how the existing pattern served us in the past, determine whether or not it serves us now in relation to who we wish to be, and if it doesn't, replace it with one that brings us into alignment with these truths.

For example, when I discovered that I worked all the time to the extent that it took me away from my family, I had to look at the source of the drive inside me to do this. I realized that my need to work all the time was rooted in a subconscious attempt to prove to my father that he had been wrong about me as a teenager. I spent ten years working myself into oblivion in an attempt to prove something to him. This was an incredible discovery for me. It was not too difficult to see how this had evolved and become ingrained in my nature. Upon this discovery, I experienced the pain of this excess baggage I was carrying around in order to reach the conclusion that I no longer needed to prove anything to anyone. It was then I decided that I wanted to be a mother whose children always came first. I wanted to establish a lifestyle in which my work schedule was secondary to my children. Now when I feel overworked, I stop and evaluate my true intentions and how I can get back on track to be who I want to be.

The most important discoveries of my life have been about who I am in my role as a mother. I realized that there was no clear design for me to pattern myself after. Our family model provides us with some direction. Society also provides us with some. The role of mothers has changed tremendously in the past twenty to forty years.

Most families require two incomes and mothers today have a great deal more on their minds than the intricate details of managing a home and children. Collectively, we are engaged in an attempt to redefine our priorities as women and still be loving, nurturing mothers. Our role seems to be in a state of flux. I realized what I needed was to disregard all the messages I received from outside sources and find my answers within.

I have discovered I am here for my children to serve as their guide.

- My job is to teach them as much as they are ready to learn from me.
- My job is to protect them from physical harm and emotional damage.
- My job is *not* to protect them from the lessons that they must learn outside of my domain.
- My job is to share unconditional love with them.
- My job is *not* to be critical, judgmental, or harsh.
- My job is to honor and nurture the spirit within them.
- My job is to allow them to learn from their mistakes.
- My job is to facilitate their growth from a child into an adult.

- My job is to assist them in the discovery of who they are.
- My job is *not* to mold them into who I wish them to be.

Knowing who I am in this relationship serves as my inner guide in every interaction between myself and my child. Do I live up to this job daily? I have to say no. There are days when I miss the mark entirely. I am aware when I have done so and I am given yet another opportunity for growth and discovery. I may not ever be perfectly who I wish to be, but there are many days and many ways that I *am* who I want to be with my children. When I am in that space, I recognize the truth of my being.

None of this happened overnight. It continues to be a lengthy process, not only for this issue, but for the many other discoveries I have made about myself. Discovering the absolute truth of my being means that I must continue to peel away the stuff that does not support the person I want to be. It is like the layers of an onion; it is best to peel one layer at a time.

Discoveries about ourselves are very life enriching. Once we become familiar with this process for ourselves, we can begin to utilize it in relation to our children. We will notice behaviors they develop for coping with situations. We cannot alter the subconscious choices our children will make about who they are. They must go through their own process of discovery. We can, however, be observant and lead them on this journey.

Our AD/HD children will no doubt establish many defenses to protect themselves from the harshness of their world. It is easy to find these defenses in a child who is rebellious, or a child who is withdrawn, or one who acts as though he no longer cares. When we see these patterns forming in our children, we can help them to discover why they are choosing to respond in a certain way. This is done through honest, nonjudgmental communication. It is important that we provide our children with the opportunity to discuss their feelings. For some, these feelings will be too painful to deal with today. Others will be able to work through their feelings with a supportive parent. The opportunity must be provided; the choice will be theirs. When the timing may not be right for them, we must let them know that we are present for them when they are ready.

We may not be able to alter the choices they make, but it does help to see why they are choosing a certain way. Then we are able to see our children with compassion and love.

If a child is making choices that are destructive to others or himself, seeking the help of a trained professional is imperative. We must be cautious not to allow our children to go down a dangerous path to self-discovery. When our observations alert us to impending danger, we must provide the necessary interventions.

I acknowledge occasions when I have not been the mother I intend to be. I always evaluate what went wrong when I did not quite make it. I discuss it with my kids when it is appropriate to do so. Then I move on. I do not beat myself up. I do not wallow in guilt.

I acknowledge myself when I have been the mother I wish to be. It feels wonderful. I am pleased with the moment and I invite many more like it. I know in these moments that this journey has been worth it.

Affirmation: I am evolving and unfolding into the perfect being that I am inside. I open my heart and allow myself to be inwardly guided in my own process of growth and self-discovery. I accept myself with compassion and love. I am patient with myself. I gently release those things about myself that are no longer useful, knowing that to everything there is a season. I joyously embrace those aspects of myself that are the true expressions of me. Today is a new day in which I experience fully the grace of becoming.

Practice

Practice makes perfect. This is true for cooking, for racquetball, and for parenting. When we are committed to being awake each day to the many opportunities before us, we make a conscious effort to be what is needed in the moment. This takes a lifetime of practice. It is a process. We cannot expect to be instantly transformed; there is too much to be learned.

As with any other skill we attempt to master, we must learn to see our parenting as a vocation. Learn to see every challenge as an opportunity to master a new skill. It may help to set a goal for each day, such as "Today I am going to practice complimenting my child."

As we practice, we make many adjustments along the way. We take notice of the emotions that are stirred within us in every situation. We become more and more aware of the issues that have made a situation seem difficult. We become better able to change our thinking and make adjustments to our parenting and teaching. During these periods of adjustment, we learn a great deal about ourselves and our children.

Sharon had struggled for years with getting Landon off to school in the mornings. Every morning, it was the same scenario. She woke Landon up, helped him organize his clothes, and left him to get dressed. She would return to check his progress only to find that he hadn't made any. After the lengthy process of getting his clothes on, Landon would then sit at the table to eat his breakfast. Sharon knew that if she left him alone with that bowl of cereal, it would never be eaten, so she would sit with him prodding him along, one bite at a time. By the time Landon left for school, Sharon was a wreck!

Then one day it occurred to her to try something new. With the help of Landon's therapist, they decided to allow Landon to get dressed in the living room, away from the distractions of his bedroom. This change proved fruitful; Landon was dressing himself in a timely manner without Sharon's constant redirection. Once free of this frustration, Sharon reviewed the breakfast procedure as well. What she noticed was her attachment to Landon completing the bowl of cereal. The one thing she had control over was her attachment. She released that attachment and gave Landon a timer with his bowl of cereal so that he could begin to learn how to manage his own time.

Once we begin to practice conscious parenting, we find that ideas for these kinds of changes become more common. As we release our own attachments and allow our children to make choices and to learn from their mistakes, we are open to an influx of ideas that honor the spirit of our child.

Patience

Patience is a necessity. To be patient with our child is every parent's goal, but we cannot have patience with our child if we have no patience with ourselves.

We must know that the parent we are is evolving, moment by moment, into the parent we intend to be. We cannot expect this to happen instantly. We are creatures of habit. Patterns that have been passed from generation to generation will not always be dissolved easily. Some of these patterns have become deeply embedded and will require time and patience to eradicate. We must be patient with ourselves when we fall short of our goals.

When we do fall short, we must learn to see the value in that. We must rejoice in the recognition that we were not who we intended to be in that moment. If we were not awake to our experience, we would not have noticed when we missed the mark. It serves no one for us to be impatient with ourselves. Having a "practice makes perfect" outlook is good modeling for our children.

Begin to see mistakes as growth opportunities instead of mistakes. A mistake is only a mistake if you fail to learn from it. Separate the major problems and the little problems and have a sense of humor about the little things.

Consciousness

My ultimate goal is to parent my children with 100 percent awareness. Ideally, I could make a conscious decision in every moment and in every situation about how I can best approach the matter before me. In every moment, I am given an opportunity to choose who I want to be. My goal is to embrace the opportunity and choose wisely.

I hope that we can all make such a commitment for our children's sake. It begins with time set aside for daily reflection. Eventually, this daily reflection becomes incorporated into the entire day. I hope that we can all reach a place where we are conscious and awake and present for our children. Then our children will be honored and valued for who they are.

In quiet moments with an awareness of the presence that is forever with us, we can reflect and grow. Taking time out of our busy schedules for such reflection is imperative. Usually, it is in our most hectic moments that we need to find a way to honor that presence. When we do, we are honoring spirit within us, and then we can begin to honor the spirit within our child.

Ten Ways to Honor the Presence Within

Be What's Missing

Often we can change the dynamics of a situation by identifying the missing components. If the situation is one of conflict and anger, we might identify the missing components as harmony and peace. We then have an opportunity to bring harmony and peace into the situation. This is done by first aligning yourself with those qualities. If it is safe to do so, remove yourself for a moment, close your eyes, breathe deeply, and become the embodiment of peace and harmony. Then, reenter the situation bringing those qualities to it. If you are unable to remove yourself, this process must take place in an abbreviated manner. You can take just a moment in the midst of the situation to do the same thing. Close your eyes, take a deep breath, and allow yourself to be infused with peace and harmony. Remove yourself mentally for just a moment, and return as these qualities. With practice, this becomes a simple process and allows you to bring spirit into the condition.

Change the Expectation

When I am not getting the results or the responses I expect from my children, I must evaluate my expectations. Many times, I have set the expectation at an unachievable level for my child. Other times, my child is having a difficult moment and is unable to meet what would otherwise be a reasonable expectation. In these situations, I have a choice: I can either maintain my expectation and the ongoing struggle to have it met or I can shift my expectation to one that my child can meet. This is difficult to do when I feel that the expectation is reasonable, but becoming stuck on my need to have it met only perpetuates the struggle. There are times when I choose not to change my expectations, but I must consciously choose. Changing the expectation, when appropriate, can eliminate the conflict.

Forgive Yourself

We spend far too much time thinking and talking about our mistakes and shortcomings. When you blow it, acknowledge it, remedy it when possible, and get over it. We do the best we can in the moment even though it may not always be our personal best. We cannot teach our children the art of forgiveness if we do not first practice it with ourselves. Our children will forgive us and we must forgive ourselves.

Know the Truth

This challenge is presented in any conflict. The truth is that nothing is permanent. In twenty years, no one will remember, or if we do, we will laugh about it. Strangers' opinions have little influence in the overall picture of our life. The sun will shine tomorrow. Dark clouds bring needed rain. This moment is not the deciding moment in my life or my child's life.

Let It Be

The serenity prayer has a lot to offer. Sometimes, even if we can change things, it isn't necessarily appropriate to do so. When you are unclear about how to proceed, let it be. When you are unhappy about a situation, let it be. You can return to it later with clarity and peace. If you are unable to change it, let it be. Give up the struggle to control every situation. If everyone is safe, let it be.

Let the Machine Pick It Up

Our lives become overwhelming at times. With all there is to do and with all the ruckus at homework time, dinnertime, and bath time, that phone call can wait. No matter who it is, you can call the person back. No matter what it is, it can wait. Allow yourself to have one less thing to do in the moment that the telephone rings. Allow yourself to be present in the moment without feeling obligated to put down the story, end the conversation, get up from the dinner table, postpone shampooing his hair, or removing her from your lap. Let the machine pick it up.

Care for Yourself

Sometimes as parents, we forget what it means to care for ourselves. We become consumed with caring for other people and other things. We care for our spouse, our children, our house, our lawn, our cars, our jobs, our bills, our obligations, and our pets. Somehow, we get left out of the equation when we should be the first variable. We must care for ourselves. We must take time to muse, to meditate, to socialize, to pamper ourselves in whatever way feels best for us. Nurture yourself, inwardly as well as physically.

Elevate Your Consciousness

Our consciousness is one of the few things we have complete control over. We have the power to choose how we will think in any situation, which in turn, determines how we will feel. We can rise above any situation in consciousness. We still have to deal with the situation, but we can choose to release our attachment to the outcome, our judgment about right and wrong, and our degree of emotional engagement. We can tune our mind into the consciousness of peace and love and then any words and actions we contribute will be given out of love and peace. Our consciousness creates our reality. Change your thinking and you will change your life.

Meditate

There are many resources available to assist you in the art of meditation. There are as many ways to meditate as there are colors. This is a process by which we clear our minds from external distractions. It allows us to become relaxed and detached. There is substantial evidence that meditation is a useful tool for healing our bodies and our minds.

Spiritual Mind Treatment

This is affirmative prayer in which you align yourself with the divine presence and recognize yourself as a part of the whole. You then affirm for yourself who you are and what your life is about, giving thanks for it knowing that it is already your truth, and releasing it.

> I recognize that there is a divine presence in the universe. It is the breath of all life. It is the essence of goodness and wholeness. It is everywhere present in every moment. I live and move and have my being within this presence. I am a creation of it. Its essence animates my being as I am one with the wholeness of this presence. I am in a divine partnership, cocreating my life with the one spirit that animates all life.
>
> My life is right now in perfect order. I am inspired and guided in all my efforts. I cannot help but blossom and grow because it is the nature of my being to do so. I nurture myself in my own growth process. I see my child as a gift from the divine source of all gifts. Wisdom and love guide me in all my parenting endeavors and I am a gift to my children. As we make this journey together, I completely accept my child for who he is and embrace my role as his guide with ease and with grace. I know

everything is unfolding just the way that it needs to. I give thanks for the opportunity to be a beacon of light for myself and for my child. I am grateful for the many gifts set before me and for the perfect unfolding of all my affairs. I release this prayer now to a power that is greater than I am, knowing that it is already done, and it is good. And so it is. And so I let it be.

8

Spiritual Parenting

Spiritual parenting means raising our children with a new awareness. It is not linked to any one religion, but can be linked to all religions. It is not about teaching our children the dogma of our personal religion; it is reaching our children through the highest means available to us—our spiritual connection.

Spiritual parenting begins with the understanding that at the purest and deepest level of existence—the spiritual level—Attention Deficit/Hyperactivity Disorder does not exist. At the level of his or her innermost being, our child remains completely free from this disorder, untouched by its challenges.

AD/HD is a neurobiological challenge. It is physical. It is not spiritual. It is not an issue of morality. While we struggle through the effects of AD/HD, we can find solace in knowing that these effects cannot even touch the spiritual aspect of our child's being.

As we practice the art of spiritual parenting, we are able to communicate with our children at a spiritual level, not merely a physical level. There are many advantages to this. Spirit is ageless, timeless, and perfect. To be able to communicate with that part of my child that is ageless, timeless, and perfect is of profound benefit to my child and to me.

This process is not psychic, or otherwise hokey. It does not require special gifts, candles, or cards. It only requires the utilization of your own spiritual connection to a higher power.

A vigilant pursuit of spirituality is sometimes seen as an unlikely possibility for parents. With so much to do, who can find time to isolate themselves in a monastery and commune with God? Any parent of an AD/HD child could find this an appealing idea, but who would take care of the kids?

While training for my practitioner's license, I was the only member of the class with young children. Others were parents, but their children were adults. Deep spiritual training requires a higher level of spiritual commitment. Parenting can easily interfere with that commitment. Even in the first few classes that I took, as we were encouraged to develop a daily practice, I found it difficult to do so because of the demands of parenting. I finally settled on the wee hours of the morning because they were the only ones left.

We all see the serious problems in our society among our youth. We can see that our children are confused, hurt, and angry. Many are killing each other in the streets and in the classroom. In our schools, the curriculum is shifting from mere academics to the teaching of values and the facilitation of healing desperately needed by our children. Our teachers are frustrated by the overwhelming demand to be so much more than they bargained for. As a society, we are stretched to our limits. Who is caring for our children?

The problems of our youth were created collectively. It is easy for us to blame other parents. It is easy for us to sit back and know that it is not our child—today. To ensure that it is not my child tomorrow, I must take preventative steps today. The steps that I choose to take with my children are of a spiritual nature. The way I impact the planet begins in my own home.

Spiritual parenting, as mentioned earlier, does not have much to do with dogma or the specific beliefs of any particular religion. Through spiritual parenting, we teach and empower our children to access a power that is greater than we are. Regardless of the dogma, most religions teach that there is such a power. Most religions teach that we have some form of access to that power. Traditional doctrines teach that we can always reach this power through prayer. New Thought philosophies teach that this power is within us, not separate from us, and that we always have immediate access to it.

By whatever means you use to access this power, I encourage you to teach your child how to rise above the physical imperfections and know the truth of their being. This truth is that at the purest level of being, they are untouched by AD/HD. This disorder offers them many opportunities to cultivate a relationship with this higher power. The development of such a relationship is a direct path to healing. It is our responsibility, as parents, to facilitate this with our children. By learning that they are untouched at this level, they are better able to confront the issues in their life and they are less overwhelmed by the challenges. It is comforting for all of us to know there is a safe port that we can always return to when the world seems to be beating up on us. We can guide our children to this safe port, the omnipresent power of the universe.

Our children are comforted by the assurance that having AD/HD is not their fault. It is not a punishment; it is not a curse. It is a challenge and an opportunity.

Our children are still taught that they must take responsibility for their conduct and the choices they make. For our children, this is a difficult concept to implant in their minds. It is worth our perseverance, however. My thirteen-year-old son does, finally, seem to understand that it is he alone who must answer for his decisions and actions.

I believe that anyone can learn the art of spiritual parenting within his or her own framework. The framework that I use has resulted in a powerful transition in the way I parent my children and I share it with you here for two reasons. The first is that my words may resonate with you and you may choose to follow a similar path. The second is that you may find a way to incorporate spiritual parenting into your own belief structure. I suggest that, though we may differ in some philosophical details, we are all arriving at a common truth.

We can teach our children that at the center of their being is a divine truth. That truth is that they are whole, perfect, and complete. We can teach them that at this center of their being they are connected to all life and to spirit, or God. At the center of their being is the answer to every question as well as the solution to any problem. This center is wholly available at all times. The way to reach this center is through quiet contemplation and prayer.

For children, brief moments of silence with a spoken meditation are very beneficial. You can lead them through a peaceful visualization. There are also meditation audiotapes that can be purchased. Sometimes, quiet time alone is all that is needed. Soft music, especially with nature sounds incorporated, also works well with children. We can teach our children to reach that connection through this calm, quiet time and manage their lives from it. They can learn that there is a divine center within that they can always return to for comfort and peace.

With prompting, my children are now able to go within and find their true self. When they are having a difficult time, I can often use simple reminders to point them in the right direction. For example, when Heather is being nasty to someone, I can whisper in her ear that I want her to take a few minutes to be alone and find her "best self." She knows that she is her "best self" when she feels connected and does not feel that tendency to be ugly to those around her. Sometimes, a reminder is all she needs and the results can be instantaneous. When she needs more, I can sit with her and hold her and we can say a prayer together. I use affirmative prayer to remind her of her connection to spirit. Occasionally, she seems to need to muddle in the "yucky stuff" for a while before she can reconnect. I will allow her to do this, but I will insist that she do it in the privacy of her bedroom and that she not impose the "yucky stuff" on to those around her. More often than not, she will return with a smile on her face or a request for help. Regardless of how we get there, she is employing the process that she has been taught to connect to a higher power and to manage her behavior from that point of connection. That is powerful stuff for a ten-year-old child with AD/HD, oppositional defiant disorder, and depression!

Love as the Foundation

Spiritual parenting provides our children with the assurance that they are always loved unconditionally. They experience this love when they go to that quiet place within and feel their connection to life. They experience this love when we work through a situation together to find the root cause of their difficulty and when they are allowed to make their own mistakes. We teach them that there is a limitless supply of love in the universe. They have access to it at all times. It is within them, it is all around them. They can experience it in a hundred different ways each day. We teach our children to experience love through their connection with God, through their connection with their family, through their connection to nature, and through their connection to the community and the world. Our children must experience this great love. It is not enough that we tell them it exists or that we tell them we love them; we must demonstrate it to them and then teach them to demonstrate this great love in their own life. When we teach our children that love is the fabric of all life, that it is the glue that holds everything together, we empower them to live a life that is free from fear of abandonment and rejection.

"Love is patient and kind. Love is not jealous or boastful or proud or rude. Love does not demand its own way. Love is not irritable, and it keeps no record of when it has been wronged. It is never glad about injustice but rejoices whenever the truth wins out. Love never gives up, never loses faith, is always hopeful, and endures through every circumstance" (1 Corinthians 13:4–7).

The Power of Choice

Choice is one of the most powerful spiritual advantages that I use with my children. Even when they seem not to have choice, they always do. They can choose to comply or they can choose not to; we all know that the child with AD/HD has a tendency toward noncompliance, be it intentional or not. By empowering our children with choice, we also encourage responsibility.

We can teach our children that there is a law of cause and effect. This law is as natural as the law of gravity. For every cause, there is an effect. For every choice they make, there is a consequence. The law of gravity has no volition. The law cannot choose to work in some instances and choose not to work in others. It works exactly the same every time regardless of who or what is involved. So it is with the law of cause and effect. There is no volition in the law. It does not choose to work in some instances and choose not to work in others. Just as every action has a reaction, every cause has an effect. Every choice we make has an effect or a consequence. When we make good choices, we usually see good effects. When we make poor choices, we usually see poor effects. By teaching our children that this is an impersonal law, they learn to see how their own choices are the cause of their reality. This is a particular challenge for a child with AD/HD. I have reaped substantial benefits using this approach with my own children and others that I have worked with. I communicate with them at a spiritual level regarding universal laws, or rules, so that they may see that it is possible to make a different choice and arrive at a different effect.

Communicating in this way eliminates a great deal of frustration for all of us. We are able to help our children determine what actions created the effects before them. We can sincerely show compassion for the consequences they must endure, but we are not responsible for their consequences. It is their own responsibility and they are able to clearly see this reality. They learn that they can make new choices to create new effects in their life. We are not the ones with the power; they are.

On the other hand, we rejoice together when what they are creating in their experience is something wonderful. In those situations, the feeling they get is enhanced tenfold because they realize that they have created this reality and have the ability to create again what they want to experience. This is the most profound responsibility as a parent—to teach our children how to create for themselves the lives they want.

The Art of Problem Solving

Problem solving with an AD/HD child can be a cumbersome process. Their perspectives often are out of sync with those of others and they often are unwilling or unable to make a shift. Spiritual parenting offers a fresh approach to problem solving.

The first step to solving any problem is determining whether or not you have a willing participant. Because we approach the situation in a state of clarity and openness, we can easily evaluate our child's willingness to find a solution. If the child is not willing to solve the problem, no matter how hard you try, you cannot force the child to be ready.

There are legitimate reasons for not being ready to solve a problem. Left alone, the situation may change drastically. Our child may have a need to experience the emotions that accompany the problem before he is able to work through the situation. We can trust in spirit to guide us and our child. When a child is obviously not ready to work through something, we have to let it go. We cannot deny him a process he needs to experience. If we do, a similar situation is sure to appear to offer him another opportunity to facilitate his personal growth.

I find that when I feel anxious to have a situation resolved, it is my own issues that are at the root of my anxiety. I am afraid for my child that if the situation is not resolved immediately, something horrible will happen. I cannot protect him from his own actions and choices. My children must make their own decisions.

We must have faith that our children are divinely protected and trust that their personal unfoldment is occurring just the way it needs to. If a child is not ready to solve a problem, honor where he is and accept it. We must release our own attachment to the immediate resolution of the problem. We have to be willing to give our child an opportunity to grow according to his own needs.

Another important component to problem solving is helping a child to see the various sides of the problem and all possible solutions. Lecturing will not work. An AD/HD child typically does not have the attention span, nor the patience, to go through a lengthy process of reviewing all the possibilities. We must ask the right questions so that he stumbles upon the answers on his own. It is important to note that sometimes the answers that my children stumble upon are not the ones that I anticipated; sometimes they are better! I can ask questions like, "What will happen if everything remains exactly the way it is now? How would you like to see things changed? What would that mean? What could you do to help make that happen? What would that look like? What would you need to do that?" After several of these kinds of questions, we can try to help them see the perspective of others by asking questions like, "How do you think she will feel if you do that? Can you think of any reason she would not want that to happen? How would it affect someone else if you did that?"

If I am uncomfortable with the answers I am receiving, most likely my child is not yet ready to work through the problem. No matter how badly I want it fixed now, I cannot force my child to be ready. If I am sure that my child is ready and I still am not comfortable with the answers I am receiving, I then have to take a break until I can get clarity on the situation. With spiritual parenting, nothing needs to be forced! There is a perfect movement of spirit through every situation and through every interaction with my child. If it doesn't feel right, I can come back to it later.

Once we help our child to explore the options and the possible effects of her choices, we then must allow her the opportunity to make her choice. Even if she makes a choice that I would rather she not make, I have to allow her to do what she feels is right for her. This is all within reason, of course. I would never allow my child to make a choice that would be harmful to herself or another. Again, I am always guided by spirit to know when and how to intervene.

Allowing our children to make their own choices is empowering them to learn life's lessons in the most effective way. They always have the love and safety of their parents to return to when the choices they make do not turn out as they had hoped. They are not met with judgment or "I told you so." There is, instead, the comfort of unconditional love and acceptance. When their choices lead to positive and productive solutions, they gain a sense of competence and confidence that can never be acquired by having their problems solved for them.

The Illusion of Mistakes

We all make mistakes. How often do we look back on a terrible mistake and realize how much good came out of it? In my own life, I look back on a period of time that I would never choose to repeat. I made decisions then that seem as though they must have been made by someone else because I cannot imagine using such poor judgment. However, it is those very mistakes that brought me to where I now am. Were they really mistakes or are they best described as growing pains? Whatever we call them, they cannot be judged solely "bad" because the end results were positive. No doubt there are experiences that we cannot see good outcomes arising from, but they are the exception and not the rule. A mistake is only a mistake if you don't learn from it and there are few mistakes that cannot be rectified.

We can teach our children that making mistakes is natural and that we always have an opportunity to learn important lessons from the mistakes we make. Spiritual parenting requires that we develop our own third eye so that we can help our children to acquire the ability to see past the immediate outcomes to the learning experience.

Some of us have to experience the same effect a hundred times or more before we can get to the learning. Have you sensed this in your AD/HD child? It is also true for countless individuals, both adults and children, without AD/HD. The greatest gift we can give a child is the ability to learn from the outcomes of the choices made in his life. For a child with AD/HD, this is an ongoing process of growth.

Spiritual parenting allows us to release our own judgments and fears and be wholly present for our child and facilitate his learning. Because we are centered and aware of our connection, we are able to sense his resistance or his openness to acknowledging the truth of the situation. We ask the right questions to guide him through a learning experience. Sometimes, he is not ready to learn, and that is okay, too. We have to set aside our own fears and judgments and allow him the opportunity to unfold according to his nature. The important thing is that we be present to facilitate this process. We offer love, support, and insight in his moments of need. We must have the ability to allow him to choose not to see what we see. We relinquish our need to convince him of what it is that we know to be true.

Affirmation: I am centered in truth and awareness and recognize my child as a child of the universe. I know that wisdom and intelligence are the true nature of his being. I allow him to make choices knowing that every choice he makes is one step on a journey of personal growth and development. I release any need to control my child's destiny and any fears for his future. I lovingly support him in his decision making process.

The Peace of Acceptance

We have been encouraged and counseled to work with a specific program to effectively change our child. Spiritual parenting is not about changing the child. The basic premise in spiritual parenting is complete acceptance of who this child is. My daughter is the sweetest, kindest, most sensitive child a person could meet. She sometimes becomes belligerent, angry, and even mean and nasty. It is not my job to change her. It is through my love, support, and guidance that she can eliminate the need to become belligerent, angry, mean, and nasty. I am certain that she will. My job is to facilitate that growth in her, not to change her. This is a complete shift in consciousness for many of us. I must be able to feel that if she never changes, that is okay. It is difficult to arrive at such complete acceptance. It is imperative that we do.

I continue to do all that I can for her in terms of treatment and medication, but I am able to see past the unattractive behaviors to the sweet, kind, sensitive child that I know she really is through and through. Because she knows that I see her in this way, she learns to see herself in this way. By seeing herself in this way, she becomes more and more the person she sees herself to be. Children see themselves through our eyes first. If looking through my eyes gives my child a beautiful picture of herself, then we cannot go wrong. If looking through my eyes presents her with anything less than a beautiful picture of herself, what basis is there for growth? My perception of her tells her that she is a growing, evolving being. She is like a beautiful flower about to blossom. If I leave that bud undisturbed and allow it to open naturally, it will blossom fully. If I try to pry apart the petals before their time, the flower will wilt and never reach its inherent potential. What the flower needs from me is sunlight and water. What my child needs from me is love and nurturing.

My assurance comes from within. I have learned to work with my children in a spiritual way and I am keenly aware of when I have acted outside of my spiritual awareness. I know because my gut feeling tells me I was not there. It happens. I move on. It becomes easier with time and practice. It becomes natural because it is natural. I know that this works because I see it in my children. I see it in their eyes, I feel it in their hugs, and I hear it in their words. I feel it in my soul. Because I honor the spirit within them, they are healthier and happier.

I do not wish to change my children. I would not even break the chains of AD/HD if it were within my power to do so. There are fewer behaviors that I would like to have changed since I began this path. Is it that my focus has shifted and I no longer need them to change, or is it that somehow they have made behavioral changes naturally as a result of this approach? I believe it is a combination of both.

I have experienced a great deal of pain over my children's difficulties through the years. Most profoundly, as a result of this practice, I have almost eliminated my pain. Over the years, I have mourned and cried about the effects of AD/HD much more than they have. This was about me, not about my children. It serves no one for me to suffer over my child's difficulties; an extreme emotional response leaves me powerless to help them.

My son Nickolas begins eighth grade this year. I am not worried about how he will do with his teachers or his peers. I have taught him what I can. I have prepared him as much as I can. He is on a journey. It is his journey. I am here for him should he need me. I continue to monitor his homework and give him reminders to help him be successful. He will have to do much of the work himself from this point on.

I hope that he can learn many of the difficult lessons about life now, before he is an adult, because I think the lessons will become more difficult later. I cannot protect him from his lessons; I cannot intervene in his outcomes. I know that he is divinely protected. A power greater than I am is guiding him through it all, even when he is not aware of it. I rejoice in knowing that he is a fabulous kid with more potential than even I can see. I am truly blessed by his presence. I learn so much about life and about myself by being his mother. It is a profound honor.

How will it all turn out? I cannot say. Will my children grow up to be happy, well-adjusted, and successful? I am certain that they will. What I do know is that I am doing the best I can for them now. I am showing them a path to wholeness. I am showing them a way to live honestly and with integrity. I am teaching them that they are inherently beautiful people in a world that is open to all possibilities. I am teaching them that they have free will and that the choices they make will create their reality. I also teach them that they have the power to change their lives. I facilitate this now and allow them the opportunity to do it on their own someday. When that time comes, I will be at peace knowing that I have given them the tools to do well. The rest is ultimately up to them.

My dream is that we all make a commitment to spiritual parenting. It is not difficult to do. Perhaps the hardest part is beginning. Where do you begin? You begin with an intention. The intention to parent from a spiritual base will set the ball in motion. The intention will sustain you when you feel you have missed the mark. The intention will lift you up when you are down and will inspire and encourage you to continue. The intent is the most important part.

In order to parent spiritually, you must first be able to define your own world in spiritual terms. If you are not already a spiritual-minded person, you may want to enroll in a class or have a series of discussions with someone who is. You may want to read some books that help you to cultivate a spiritual perspective. You may seek out a church community that draws out your sense of spirituality.

You must also be able to clearly define where you end and your child begins. This can come only when we are honest with ourselves about our own pain and the source of our pain. A lot of healing takes place when we make these discoveries. Until we begin this process, we easily confuse our own inner issues with the issues confronting our children.

If you are fortunate enough to have a spouse who is willing to take these steps with you, this is an invaluable opportunity for both of you. So often a spouse can see things in us that we are unable to see in ourselves. They sometimes see when we are becoming the parent we said we never would long before we notice it. They see some of the connections between our parenting and our old wounds. If we can agree to listen to one another about these things, we can experience incredible growth together.

Once you begin this process, you find that it does not end. There is always a thirst for more. There is no greater experience than opening your heart to the divine influx of love and truth. The more I know, the more I want to know. The more I experience, the more I need to experience. The more I read, the more I want to read. Each discovery leads me on a new path. Each insight lights a new spark within me.

There is a creative urge within every one of us to become more, to be more. Inherent in each of us is that special something that is constantly seeking greater expression. This something is spirit, which is all that we are and at the same time greater than we are. There is a divine urge within every one of us to be the very best parent there is! The pattern of perfection lies at the center of our own being and it unfolds in us as we allow it to do so.

There is a reason that your AD/HD child is with you. You and your child are on a beautiful journey together. It does not have to be riddled with pain and crisis. It can, instead, be a fabulous journey of love and enlightenment. You can experience in yourself, and with your child, the joy of becoming.

9

The Key to a Successful School Year

While at the swimming pool, visiting with other moms, I observed a most peculiar incident. A nineteen-month-old boy accidentally bumped his head on the side of the pool. He looked up inquisitively and then deliberately threw his forehead into the concrete with brute force. I realized later that this is a perfect analogy for what we are doing in educating children with AD/HD. We continuously beat our heads against the concrete, so to speak, in an effort to reshape the child.

Our children continue to behave in a certain way to see if the behavior will result in a different outcome this time. It has been said that a child with AD/HD will repeat a behavior time and time again based on the memory of the one time out of a hundred that the behavior paid off. Whereas, a child without AD/HD is more likely to refrain from repeating the behavior based on the knowledge that ninety-nine times out of a hundred the behavior does not pay off.

Are we, as parents and teachers, doing the same thing? Do you find yourself repeating a behavior with your child in the hope that this time your behavior will pay off, even though it never has before? "This time my yelling about his fidgeting will cause him to stop forever. This time, after giving him a sequence of instructions, he will remember each one. This time, without a reminder, he will remember to take his medication. Today, the medication will change him completely. This time . . ." One of the most important things I have learned is that when I feel as though I am beating my head against a concrete wall, I am not doing something right. Either there is another way to approach the situation or my child is not yet ready to change the behavior.

There is a difference between behavior management and a continuous effort to stop or change a behavior. When we give up the struggle to change or stop a behavior and instead focus on management of that behavior, we are faced with a much simpler task. For simplicity, let us use the example of pencil tapping. It is a minor but annoying behavior seen in many of our children. Many teachers find this behavior impossible to tolerate. My son is aware that he fidgets, but is not aware that he is doing so in the moment. One strategy for this is to give the child a pipe cleaner to tap instead of the pencil. Another is to speak privately with the student and request that he find another, less disruptive, outlet for his energy. I have told Nickolas that when his fidgeting is not an overt imposition to the people around him (when it is not loud), the irritation experienced by others is about themselves. If he is asked not to fidget, he is then aware that it is bothering someone else and he can evaluate whether or not he can find a less obvious release for his pent-up energy. He has been made aware that his fidgeting can be a source of irritation for others. We have explored the different types of fidgeting and identified those least annoying and explored the possibilities for changing the type of fidgeting based on a request. I do not see any real probability that he will be able to stop fidgeting. Since he is unable to change the behavior, the best thing to do is to work with him to manage it. Acknowledging this, and giving up the struggle to change him, I then become proactive in helping him to be the best expression of who he is.

Reality Check

The first step is to recognize what the child is capable of. Many times we ask the child with AD/HD to do something that he is quite simply unable to do. We do this at home and at school. In school, we continue to seat the student with AD/HD at a desk, with an assignment, and expect him to perform like the other students. At the end of class, most students are finished, or nearly so, and the AD/HD student has barely begun. So, the incomplete assignment is sent home with the mistaken expectation that he will complete it at home. Several other teachers have had a similar experience with this student today, so he will take home four incomplete class assignments along with the three homework assignments all other students take home.

This child is motivated to do the work. He finishes his responsibilities at home and then sits down at 4:30 P.M. to tackle the four assignments that he could not finish in class and the three that he has for homework. It takes him thirty minutes or so to clean off his desk and get the assignments out of his notebook (assuming he can now find them) and another fifteen minutes to decide which assignment to do first. At some point during this forty-five minutes, he becomes overwhelmed by all this mess and takes a ten-minute break. About that time, Mom or Dad comes into the room and yells at him, "What the heck are you doing? You've been in here for an hour and you haven't done one thing! No wonder you have all this homework. No wonder your grades are so bad! No wonder you drive your teachers crazy. You know you'll never get into a good college like this. How are you going to function in life? You better get all this work done!"

Now he is in no mood for schoolwork at all, but fearing his parents' wrath, he tries to get to work. He works for about ten minutes and someone alerts him that it is dinnertime. Dinner takes an hour. It is 7:00 P.M. now and he has four incomplete assignments and three homework assignments and bedtime is 8:00 P.M. He has completed nothing. So, he goes back into his room to get some work done. He knows he cannot get it all done, but he wants to, so he tries. He works for a few minutes and then wonders where he put that baseball card he borrowed from Joey, so he takes a short break to look for it. Thirty minutes later, he still has not found it. Mom or Dad come in to check on his homework progress and, horrified to find him still off-task, they yell again. Once more he sits down to work. He manages to complete one of the incomplete assignments! It is now 8:15 P.M. He is tired and he wants to go to bed, but he has three incomplete assignments and three homework assignments. No one is happy with his performance, least of all himself.

By now, you are probably laughing or crying at the familiarity of this situation. We have repeated this scenario so many times in our home that we know it well. Then you go to a school conference and the teachers tell you that they do not understand why he never does his homework. They tell your child that if he only tried harder and cared more, he could do it. They have never watched him try. It can be futile to try to convince them of his good intentions.

We are all banging our heads against the concrete in this scenario. The classroom teacher is doing so by repeating the same expectations without modifications. The parents do so by allowing the classroom expectations to continue and by expecting that today some miraculous transformation will occur within the brain of this child and he will be able to do today what he could not do yesterday. Every time this child attempts to do the impossible, he, too, beats his head against the concrete.

I assure you that my son is more resilient than I am. I assure you that he has a higher commitment to his education than I ever had. School was easy for me and I rarely had homework. I was a kid who finished everything in class, including the homework. I did not have to study for tests. Everything came pretty easy to me. The teachers wished that I would talk less, but they could not really complain too much about a talkative honor student. If I had to struggle the way my son does, I am sure I would have given up. To this day, I do well those things that come easily to me and I avoid those things that do not. I believe this to be true for most of us. I have enormous respect for my child. There are days when he lies on his bed and cries. Most of the time, his tears are justified. Most days, he presses forward. His attempts to remain academically sound come at a high price. He has very little free time during the school year. All of his time is devoted to schoolwork and chores. Occasionally, he gets tired of it all and slacks off. Then there is a meeting and we have to get back on track. I am sure I do not tell him enough how much I admire his staying power. I am the only one ever to acknowledge this about him.

I suggest that we place too high a value on academic prowess. Not everyone can be an A or B student. Many very successful adults made C's and D's all the way through school. I am not suggesting that our kids should not try to do well in school, but I am suggesting that high grades should not be the sum total of their self-worth or a supposedly accurate prediction of their future.

The Best Teacher for the Job

In order for the AD/HD child to experience success in the classroom, many factors must be in place. Most are completely out of his control. First and foremost to classroom success is a compassionate teacher who is knowledgeable about AD/HD. This is the foundation for the child's classroom success. Our teachers must receive education and training about Attention Deficit/Hyperactivity Disorder. If our schools are not providing the necessary information, the job of educating the teachers is deferred to the parent of the AD/HD child. The teacher must understand the disorder and what the child is capable of doing and be willing to meet our child where he is when he walks in the door. We cannot expect more from him than he is capable of. Teachers must stop comparing our children to their non-AD/HD peers. Teachers must not worry about fairness. True fairness means that every child has what she needs to be successful.

My son, Nickolas, has a very difficult time with handwriting. He is very creative and linguistically gifted, but he was not performing in the content area of written language in third grade. We met with the teachers, principal, counselor, my husband, and myself to discuss our concerns. It was hypothesized that the writing deficiency most likely stemmed from his difficulties with handwriting. The solution agreed upon was for Nickolas to use the typewriter for his written assignments.

Two days later, we received a letter in the mail from his teachers that said that in order to maintain a democracy within the classroom, Nickolas would not be allowed to use the typewriter. He would, in fact, be treated like every other student. It was unfair, in their estimation, to allow Nickolas to type his assignments when the other students had to write theirs by hand.

These teachers missed the point entirely! The issue did not in any way affect the other students. The issue was strictly about this child. It was about providing this child with a simple tool that would help him to be more successful in the classroom. It was unfair to deny him the tool he needed to succeed.

The issue of fairness surfaces often in regard to assignment modifications. Math is a good example. Nickolas is extremely talented in math. There are no special programs for him, so he has to do the same math, more or less, as his peers. He knew how to do the math correctly before he walked in the door or shortly thereafter. He is given an assignment of forty math problems to be completed by tomorrow. He has some class time to work on the assignment and the remainder of the work must be finished at home. This is an impossible task for a child with AD/HD. It has nothing to do with whether or not he knows the material. He probably will not complete the assignment because he is unable to remain focused on the task. He could probably complete an assignment of twenty problems. That would be a challenge and would probably take Nickolas the same amount of time his peers would spend on forty problems. Many teachers view assigning fewer problems as an unfair advantage over the other students. Again, it has nothing to do with the other students. The AD/HD child is already at an unfair disadvantage by the nature of the disorder. Modifying the assignment only levels the playing field.

A compassionate classroom teacher who is willing to work with the AD/HD student can provide him every opportunity to achieve. She must be willing to shorten assignments, refrain from sending home incomplete assignments, help the student to self-monitor, and provide constant, positive feedback to both the student and his parents. Some commonly used classroom strategies are listed in Appendix B. The following basic guidelines for classroom teachers have been found to be effective with AD/HD students:

- Acknowledgment
- Personal feedback

- Reasonable expectations
- Identification of strengths
- Home/school partnership
- Establishment of goals, rewards, and incentives

Let's look at these guidelines, one by one.

Acknowledgment

Students need acknowledgment of the disorder and the difficulties they encounter because of it. They need to know their teacher is aware of their AD/HD and how it affects them in the classroom. Oftentimes, I hear teachers say that these kids use AD/HD as an excuse. I suggest that most of the time they are not doing that. In my experience, they are using AD/HD as a valid explanation for their difficulties. We know that this disorder affects a person's ability to perform in certain ways; it is not an issue of willingness, but of ability. Our role as teachers and as parents is to validate the explanation and be solution-oriented.

A good example is the student who has forgotten to take his medication. Any parent or teacher who has worked with a kid who takes meds knows that it can be disastrous when they forget. My own son has been in this situation. Many times he was told that having forgotten his meds was not an excuse for his behavior. This is true: It is not an *excuse* for anything. It is, however, a valid *explanation* for why he is bouncing off the walls, why he has completed nothing, and why he is having difficulties interacting with his peers. Nickolas eventually became afraid to tell his teachers when he had forgotten his meds because he dreaded their response.

I encourage teachers always to ask their students with AD/HD to inform them right away if they have forgotten their medicine. I see this as information that can be extremely useful. The student should not hear the "It's no excuse" lecture. Instead, the opportunity to discuss what needs to happen should be seized. We can determine what we, as teachers, can do to accommodate our AD/HD students and make it easier for them to get through the day. We can then make requests of them that would be helpful to us. We can establish a private signal of some sort that communicates to them, or vice versa, that things are getting out of control. I always find this to be a win-win situation. In this interaction, we honor the experience our student is having with our response. We respond with compassion and understanding. We make having a good day the priority. Most often, the student who forgot his meds is dreading the day. If we respond with that same dread, surely we set the stage for dreadful things to happen. A successful day is more important than whatever assignment we had planned. I do not necessarily recommend excusing them from their classroom assignment, but I do suggest working with them to make plans for how to get it done. When our students know they can count on us for compassion and understanding, we can count on them for honesty and their best effort.

One of my students with AD/HD, Tom, walked into my first-period class one morning with his hair standing straight up, a mustache of milk on his face, and a frazzled look in his eyes. The boy who walked in with him was admonishing him for being annoying, and I knew immediately that something was very wrong. As the students took out their materials and prepared for the day, Tom shuffled papers and books aimlessly. I quickly gave the class something to do and asked Tom if he could run an errand for me. He looked at me with utter surprise. Within earshot of other kids, I told Tom that I had an important job that I needed help with. We stepped out into the hallway and I shared my observations with Tom. Tears welled up in his eyes as he began to tell me that he just didn't know what was wrong with him. "I'm just no good at anything," he said. He had had an argument with his mom before school, his sister had hidden his baseball mitt, he'd almost missed the bus, and then his new girlfriend had acted like she didn't know him. Things were going very badly and it was only 7:45 A.M. I listened and validated his feelings. When he had gotten it all out, I asked him if he had remembered to take his medication. The tears began to well up again as he said, "No, and now it's only going to get worse." I told Tom to go to the bathroom, wet his hair and comb it out, wash his face, and then take a walk around the track until he felt like returning to class. He started to walk away and asked, "Ms. Young, what was the job you wanted me to do for you?" I explained to him that the very important job was for him to take care of himself and regroup.

Tom returned twenty minutes later, having missed most of my class. When class ended, I gave him an abbreviated version of that day's assignment and gave him two days to turn it in. We talked about ways he could make it through the day and I offered to be available throughout the day if things started to go in the wrong direction. I also told him to tell his other teachers, privately, that he had forgotten his meds and would need a little more help than usual. Tom checked in with me at the end of that day and said that it had been tough, but he had gotten through the day.

Eventually, we were able to make arrangements with Tom's mother and physician for him to take his morning medication at school. This is often a viable solution for students who occasionally forget to take their medicine before leaving home. Even if there are only a couple of doses in the nurse's office for those occasional mishaps, the benefits are immeasurable. A forgotten dose can spell disaster for many of our students.

Rarely have I had a student use AD/HD as an excuse for any behavior or inadequacy. I think that by handling situations with respect and open communication, my students have learned that they can have a good day even if they forget to take their medicine. We have an opportunity to honor the spirit of our students by acknowledging the presence of AD/HD and by validating the affects of this disorder.

Personal Feedback

We all benefit from feedback and we are constantly searching for it. We observe the body language of those we interact with, we listen to the tone of their voice, and we pick up on the energy being exchanged. The feedback we receive either feels good or not-so-good. We also seek verbal feedback. We want our friends and family to tell us what they think about what we are doing. We especially want positive feedback.

AD/HD children need a great deal of feedback. They are

not as sensitive to nonverbal cues as others are. They know when the energy exchange between themselves and a teacher is not good. They can tell by the tone of voice, the body language, and other nonverbal cues. They may not be proficient at consciously interpreting such clues, but the feeling of acceptance or rejection is generated. When the nonverbal feedback communicates a feeling of acceptance, then verbal feedback can be exceptionally beneficial.

Feedback can be delivered in the form of a teacher's position in the room in relation to the student. This is commonly referred to as proximity control. When lecturing, for example, if there is a student who is in some way being disruptive, there are two things a teacher can do that are very effective. The first is to simply walk over to the student while continuing to speak to the class and stand very near him for a couple of minutes, then move away from him again. Usually, the student will not continue the disruptive behavior for long. If this hovering presence is not enough, a light tap on his desk may be needed to convey the message. If this still is not enough, it may be necessary to pause briefly and whisper a request to him. This does not require any time or attention away from the other students.

The second technique is to simply stop talking. It does not take long before the student will notice that the drone of the teacher's voice is gone and he will look up and know what he needs to do. If a problem persists with a particular student, simply stating that we will need to talk briefly after class will likely motivate him to silence. I try to use the after-class meeting as a last resort, because by that time the student is no longer hearing what is going on in class. For the remainder of the class, he is thinking about the meeting after class.

It is important to remain very calm and be careful not to attack the student when a situation seems to have escalated. It is not necessary to argue with a student. At times, the feedback that is required is "This is not acceptable!," which is followed by a consequence for the behavior. The end result will likely be mutual respect and a working relationship. Teachers must have clearly defined rules and boundaries. We honor the spirit of the student by clearly stating the expectations and not allowing the boundaries to move. Our difficulties often lie with our expectations.

It is sometimes necessary for a student to be removed from the classroom. I recommend this only be done in instances when the behavior must be addressed by a school administrator or when the teacher is unable to continue teaching the class because of a student's disruptive behavior. Although students with AD/HD may need to be sent out of the classroom occasionally, I do not recommend that it become a frequent occurrence.

When we cultivate a mutual trust and respect with a student, they will come to rely on our feedback. Daily reports are a fabulous way to provide feedback to a student. At the end of each class period the teacher and student have an opportunity to review and rate the student's performance in certain areas. This type of feedback works well on a rating scale of 1 to 5. It should be predetermined what tasks and behaviors will be rated each day. For younger students, no more than three and for older students no more than five items should be included. There are many different report forms available. I prefer a personalized report. See Appendix A for examples of daily reports.

The best feedback is private and personal. I once had a teaching situation in which I had a free period I could use to meet briefly with my students one on one. The results were overwhelmingly positive. One AD/HD student I worked with had had a horrible school experience the previous year. She and I were able to cultivate a mutual respect and trust. I met with her privately and allowed her to talk about her experiences in an environment of acceptance and safety. She could say anything she wanted to about her school experience and I would listen without judgment. I would often ask her if she was ready to have a different experience and if she was able to hear a suggestion. I did not impose my suggestions on her. I soon found that she wanted to hear them and did try to incorporate them into her interactions and responses. I would call her in to see me three times a week at the beginning of the year, then twice a week, and finally once a week. She could request a meeting with me at any time. The other teachers were amazed at the difference the meetings made in this student. Regular meetings with my AD/HD students became a beneficial vehicle for providing feedback, enhancing their self-esteem, their sense of empowerment, and their school success. I recognize that this free period was an anomaly and most teachers do not have such an opportunity. Ideally, our school administrators at the highest level will realize this as a necessity and begin funding time for one-on-one counseling or monitoring of AD/HD students. Meanwhile, teachers who wish to be truly effective with their AD/HD students must maneuver creatively to find such time for them.

The most important component to feedback is that it must be honest, positive, and as immediate as possible. That is not to say that we should not discuss negative aspects of their performance. It is to say, however, that the intent behind our feedback must always be positive. We must learn to approach negative situations with a positive attitude. We must always build good upon good. Always dish out much more praise than criticism. AD/HD students who are praised for improvement will continue to improve. When their improvement is not noted and acknowledged, they are easily discouraged and begin to think that their efforts are not worth it.

Reasonable Expectations

So much time is wasted expecting these children to do the impossible. Unreasonable expectations set the stage for disappointment and disaster for everyone involved. I have seen many teachers depleted by their unsuccessful efforts to effect changes that are not possible. I have seen so many kids with AD/HD depleted by the relentless burdens placed upon them. I have also seen many, many parents of AD/HD children discouraged by the day-in and day-out struggle to help their children be successful in school using standards that are not realistic for their child.

In order to establish reasonable expectations, it is imperative that we are observant of the student's levels of performance academically, behaviorally, and socially. Documentation is necessary to determine a baseline. Once we know the level of performance, we can initiate a plan for improvement. Improvement should always be the goal, not perfection. I think a reasonable goal for improvement is 20 percent above baseline. Therefore, if I determine that a student is completing 30 percent of each assignment on average, I can then establish a goal of 50 percent completion. I would then modify the assignments given to this student so that I am requesting that he do half of the regular assignment for full credit. For example, if Charlie completes only three of the ten spelling words on his spelling assignment each week, I would reduce his word list to five. When he completes all five, he will receive full credit. It is important to remember this is about Charlie becoming successful, not about what other students are required to do.

Once the student is successful with the modified assignment for a three-week period, we can then increase the expectation by another 10–15 percent. Charlie would then be given six words each week. With this procedure, we can build on success, adding responsibility incrementally. This will not happen overnight. With the expectations at 20 percent above baseline, the AD/HD student still must work diligently to be successful. This technique allows the student to experience success. If, at any time, the student begins to feel overwhelmed, you will see a slide in performance back to baseline, or less.

It is important to be positive in our approach to modifying assignments. We do not want to deliver the information in such a way that the student or his family feels that he is a failure. The issue must be approached in such a way as to acknowledge the difficulties the student is having and provide a way for him to work toward competency.

The long-range goal is to have the student become capable of handling a regular workload. Do not be disappointed if the student does not reach a point in which modifications are no longer needed. They will probably be necessary for a long time. With modifications, love, and encouragement, these kids can be honor students with scholarships to good colleges and universities. They can be the cream of the crop.

Susan's son, Jerry, is an inspiration. Susan could write her own book about him, for his is indeed a success story. Jerry, a quiet young man with AD/HD, is now a junior in college. He had difficulties throughout elementary school and an especially difficult time in middle school, or junior high.

Jerry remembers a time when he had a teacher with whom he clashed terribly. He was constantly being sent to do his work in the office. After several attempts at negotiation, Susan demanded that Jerry be moved to another teacher's class. The new classroom experience was more successful and Jerry gained a sense of pride that his mom cared enough to have him moved. More important than changing classes was the message that he was not the one who needed to be changed. The expectations needed to be changed, not Jerry.

Jerry's parents never gave up on him. They loved him and supported him through what were, undoubtedly, very painful times for the entire family. Jerry came through it all beautifully. He went on to a private high school where he did very well. He now attends Arizona State University and has done quite well there. Although he was medicated when younger, he no longer chooses to take medication. He is a wonderful person. Jerry has publicly acknowledged his parents for their undying support and confidence in him as his source of strength to overcome the difficulties of having AD/HD. I admire Susan and her husband for the fine job they have done raising him and I know that they wish they had a dollar for every person Jerry has proven wrong. When I am having difficult times with my children, Susan is one of my favorite people to talk to because our conversations have a meaningful connection. She listens to me and remembers her own turbulent times. I listen to her and know that my own turbulence is only temporary.

It is reasonable to expect our students with AD/HD to show up with a good attitude and be the best they can be. It is reasonable to expect them to be respectful. It is reasonable to expect improvement. It is also reasonable to expect them to become discouraged from time to time. Honoring the spirit of AD/HD children means that we allow them to unfold as the person that they are. We are available to offer guidance and support. We accept them for who they are and help in the best way possible. We talk with them and we listen to them. We hear their fears, their perceptions, their hopes and dreams. We love them. We know that there is much more to life than being a student and we know that this child as "student" is only a small part of who they are. We remember that what we see today is only a snapshot of their total experience.

It is not reasonable to expect the student with AD/HD to look like the other students in the classroom. It is not reasonable to expect them to produce what the other students produce. It is not reasonable to expect them to become who they are not. It is not reasonable to assume that if they would only try harder, they would do better. Trying harder will most likely not result in doing better.

Establishing reasonable expectations is essential to the development of the AD/HD child as a "student." With unreasonable expectations, either the student and the adults involved will continue to spin their wheels with few gains, or the student will shed his "student" identity and give up altogether. We honor the spirit within the child when we accept him for who he is, as he is. We cannot expect him to be someone he is not.

Identifying Strengths

Each of us is born with unique talents and strengths. It is really not difficult to identify the strengths of an AD/HD student. You may have to look outside your current definition of "student" to see those strengths. These kids typically have a good deal of energy. They can be very creative. Many of them like to be helpers; they love running errands. They can do well with organizational tasks.

For example, my son loves to organize other people's things. He is not too keen on getting any of his own things organized, but will spend hours organizing our CD rack. Every classroom, school library, or school cafeteria has some kind of organizing task readily available for the AD/HD student who needs a change of pace or a positive experience, even if it is the bookshelf that you just organized yesterday. These children are often competent at running errands. These types of strengths should be identified in order to provide controlled positive experiences as needed.

There are also more significant strengths to be acknowledged, the ones that are easily overlooked. Because our kids do not usually match up to the typical definition of "good" student, they seldom receive acknowledgment for their inner talents. My son is respectful, sensitive, curious, kind, and persistent. My daughter is sensitive, deliberate, fair, and funny. None of these words are written in their cumulative folders or on any report card. These traits are just as important as other more academic skills they may not have mastered.

By identifying strengths, we are able to build on them to facilitate more success. It is too often true that we are able to quickly identify a student's weaknesses or shortcomings, but when pressed for strengths, our list pales in comparison. We all work better when others recognize our good qualities. There is good in everyone. There is something magnificent in each child with AD/HD. We must identify that magnificence and build on it.

I once had a student who was absolutely unable to complete any paper and pen task. Additionally, he was hyperactive beyond comprehension. He had extremely poor social skills and, because he got himself off to school in the mornings, had a very unkempt appearance. I knew I had to identify some strengths to build on. What I found is that verbally, he could answer any question. His comprehension was above average and he understood things that other students did not. I tried having him work with another student, with him supplying the way to write things and the other student doing the writing, but his social difficulties interfered with that process. Eventually, what I found worked best was having him verbalize his answers instead of writing them down. I did not excuse him from written work because I feel it is a crucial skill to develop and one that is definitely within my scope of work to attempt to teach. However, many of his assignments were verbal so that he had opportunities to be successful.

For another student who had great difficulty completing written work, I identified his strength in verbal problem solving and found that he could write a couple of sentences, come to my desk to talk with me about the sentences, identify his own mistakes, and then return to his desk to correct them. He was able to complete written work by having very frequent opportunities to get out of his seat and talk about his work as he did it.

Home-School Partnership

The most influential people in any child's life are his parents. To build success in the classroom, it is imperative that parent involvement be established. Parents have much more to offer than many teachers realize.

First and foremost, they know their kids. They have the benefit of knowing what works well with their child and what does not work well. They have been there for the previous years' experiences and can offer insights for teachers to avoid the pitfalls of the years past. They also have a direct line with the child that teachers cannot establish. Parents often know more than teachers will ever know about what motivates their child. They know his hurts and his joys. They know his fears and his confidence. They are witness to his truest reaction to his classroom experiences.

A teacher once pointed out to me that my child was not concerned about his lack of success in her classroom. She said that he was not motivated to do well in school. I quickly pointed out to her that she had no idea to what extent my child was affected by the events in her classroom. He did not feel safe, in her presence, to express the truth of his being. He did not feel safe to express his pain. He cried daily at home because of what was happening within the confines of her domain; her assumption that she had a view into my child's soul was grossly inaccurate.

As teachers, we must guard against this way of thinking. A child is never unaffected by his classroom experience. We may not be able to see the effects, but usually the parents do. Communication with parents offers us vital information about how the student is reacting emotionally to our strategies. It is also imperative that we know how homework is being done at home. It is not safe to assume that if the work is getting done, everything is okay. Getting the work done is only part of the equation. What is the effect on the student and the family?

How long does it take? How much assistance is required? Does this child have time to be a kid? What is the family experiencing? We must have this information to carve a path that leads to improvement and success. Otherwise, we are working on blind assumptions.

It is one thing to talk about building partnerships with parents; it is quite another thing when we run into a parent who really wants that partnership. I have been told that I am too involved in my son's education. I completely disagree. I am intimately aware of my child's growth areas, academically and otherwise. My child's progress cannot be separated into school and not school. He and I chart the waters together, so to speak. He is taking over the role of captain, more and more, and I the first mate. We are still together on this ship. The beautiful thing about him being thirteen is that I have the benefit of his feedback. He still needs and wants my support. I try not to shelter him from his lessons.

We have had some pretty bad experiences in the educational arena. It is my job to help him put those experiences into perspective and not to incorporate the negative feedback into his self-image. It is my job to help him identify those things about himself that he needs to work on in order to have a more pleasant experience.

I want to know what is going on in the classroom. I want to know what work he is to complete at home. I want to know what long-term assignments are hanging out there. I want to be informed of his progress throughout the term. I want to provide information to the teacher about my child to facilitate the best possible experience for him in the classroom. I do not want to tell the teacher how to teach, only how to best work with my child.

Establishing Goals

When establishing goals for a student with AD/HD, it is important to consider both academic and behavioral goals. Goals should be broken down into long- and short-term. Always keep in mind that the student with AD/HD has a difficult time with long-term goals. They function best with immediacy. Short-term goals are stepping stones to long-term goals. Establish a small number of goals to avoid overwhelming everyone concerned. Establish a means of feedback that is quantitative and immediate. Involve the student, parents, other teachers, school administrators, and other professionals working with the student.

Academic goals for students with AD/HD typically include assignment completion, organization, neatness, and accuracy. When considering an academic goal for assignment completion, it is imperative to establish a baseline, as discussed earlier in this chapter. A goal for assignment completion without a modification in the length of the assignment will probably fail to yield positive results.

Organization is one of the most significant difficulties for these students. It is too much to ask that the parents alone take responsibility for helping the student to be organized. There are many opportunities throughout the school day to help the student improve organizational skills. Students can be assigned buddies to assist each other with organization. This can be set up in an enjoyable way that does not embarrass any particular student. Students can be asked to trade notebooks and try to locate the necessary items for completing tonight's assignment. Other ideas include having the teacher check to see that everything the student needs is physically present, an assignment notebook for parents and teachers to sign off on, and class time to organize papers.

Accuracy can also be an area of difficulty for students with AD/HD. Some students have little difficulty completing assignments, but rush through them so quickly that their accuracy is minimal. These students can also benefit from reductions in assignments to teach them to work more slowly and carefully and to recheck their work.

Deciphering the work of these students is a challenge for the most talented among us. Handwriting is typically very hard to read, as are numbers. It is important to experiment with different writing implements, different paper, and different formats to find what works best for each student. Students should be allowed to sharpen their pencils often to increase neatness. Mechanical pencils may enhance neatness. Having students recopy messy work is seldom effective, and since time is of the essence, this is counterproductive. Minimizing the amount of written work seems to increase neatness also. As much as possible, avoid having these students copy.

Behavioral goals will vary greatly depending on the individual needs of the student. Some students may need goals regarding student-teacher interactions. Others may not. Many students with AD/HD will need behavioral goals regarding social skills. Common classroom behavior goals include task completion, working quietly, and speaking out only when called upon. It is important to determine what behavioral goals will be used and then spend a week or more collecting information on the student's current level of performance. Establish a baseline and then set goals for improvement.

Whether you are establishing academic or behavioral goals, or a combination thereof, it is imperative that they be few in number. Too many goals are difficult for the adults to administer and difficult for the student to achieve. The primary goal should always be success. We want our students to reach the goals that are established. Depending on the student's needs and the age of the student, three to five goals is usually an appropriate number. Make sure that the goals are measurable and the student understands what meeting the goal looks like.

Rewards and Incentives

In a perfect world, each one of us would do the things that we need to do without any thought to what was in it for us. We would do our job for the sheer pleasure and satisfaction of it. However, most of us work for rewards and incentives, and there is nothing wrong with doing so.

Money, of course, is the primary motivator in our society. Most of us get up each morning and do what we do anticipating that we will be paid for our work. How long would you stay with your current employer if he told you that the company would no longer be willing to pay you, but they hope that you will stay on without pay? We work for money and for bonuses. Many companies offer company cars for top sales producers. Cash bonuses are still used as incentives. One company I worked for issued a bonus that could not be cashed in for three years; this was their way of rewarding employees for a job well done and offering an incentive to stay with the company at the same time. Sometimes, we work for the vacation that we will be able to take in a few more months. We all receive bonuses and incentives in some form.

It should be no different for students. Many students are content to work for grades. The letters shown on the report card are sufficient for them. For students with AD/HD, the report card is too long-term and the A is too difficult to achieve. So, we need to provide other rewards and incentives. These must be individualized to gain optimum results. The student and parents should be involved in the planning of rewards and incentives.

There are many effective rewards that are often overlooked. Time with adults is a rare commodity for today's child. Our classrooms are typically overcrowded and personalized attention is rare. Our families typically consist of working parents who are pressed for time and energy. Children today do not have many opportunities to spend quality time alone with an adult. I have found that students with AD/HD will work for this kind of time. Kids will work to have lunch with a teacher. They will work to have a special activity with Mom or Dad. They will work to be a helper to an administrator that they like. Our kids love individualized attention and they will work for it!

Creating rewards and incentives between school and home is another very effective tool. You can easily develop a system of communication between teachers and parents that is conducive to a home-school contingency plan. That is, when the student performs in a specific way at school, there are rewards or consequences enforced at home. This is essential to a successful program. This sets the stage for a true partnership between parents and teachers. It is imperative that home-school communication includes as much, if not more, positive feedback as negative. Too much emphasis on negative aspects of the student's experience depletes the student and the parents of energy to continue with the program. By emphasizing the positive, we honor the spirit of the child by acknowledging all the good that is within him. If we cannot focus on the good, then we are not honoring the child. There is always good to be found. Even in a classroom for emotionally and behaviorally challenged students, there is good to be found in each student. The more focus put on the beneficial qualities of the student, the more the student will relate to those qualities and develop them further.

The student with AD/HD will also work for a break! This is a great incentive for students with difficulty completing assignments. Offer them a break after a certain amount of work is completed. While they are on break, you can check the accuracy of their work. The break can be short and should not exceed the amount of time it took them to complete the work. For a student who is struggling through a written assignment, after he completes five sentences, he can have a five-minute break. You must establish parameters for the break. The student must be aware that if he interferes with other students who are working, his break ends. This should be clear to the student before he is given the opportunity to earn a break.

Students on a daily report system should have daily or weekly incentives, depending on their specific needs. Daily reports that include a rating system can easily be used to establish long-term goals, such as offering an incentive if so many points are earned within a certain time frame. Again, a baseline should be established, and the goals should always be for improvement, not perfection.

I encourage teachers and parents to be creative with rewards and incentives. Knowing the child gives you much insight into what will work for a particular student. Be observant and the perfect idea will jump out at you. You will see what the student's interests are. Sometimes finding a motivator for a student is difficult. This is especially true for older students with a history of failure. We must remain committed to identifying a motivator. Keep in mind, constantly, the fact that every child is motivated by something.

When Nothing Seems to Work

Under the best of circumstances, no teacher can feel successful with every student. Despite all the emphasis that I have placed on helping kids with AD/HD, there have been a few such students for whom I was still not able to find the right strategies.

It is a challenge even when all the pieces of the puzzle are on the table, but when one or more essential pieces are missing, the degree of success is lessened. Sometimes, an understanding and willing teacher is the missing link. Sometimes, an available parent is the missing piece. Sometimes, the student has given up. Almost always, there are so many other students with needs of their own that we are somewhat limited in our ability to help a particular child. Whatever the missing link is, it is not productive to assign blame.

Regardless of what is missing, those who are available to the student must continue to do what we can do to honor the spirit of the child. Regardless of the appearance, we must remember that what we see is a snapshot of this student, not a portrait. This student has a lifetime to evolve and become more of who and what he will be as an adult. It is not imperative that we mold him into a responsible adult today. This student has many lessons to learn and we cannot know how he will learn them best. We can offer our unconditional recognition of the spirit within him. We can know that regardless of the appearances, this student is and will always be a divine being. This student is right now all that he needs to be. We can ask ourselves if we are being all that we can be in relation to the student, as he is today.

Often, the emphasis is on the student and the "problems" caused by the student. Really, these kids offer us many more opportunities than we realize. We easily forget that we are given an opportunity to grow and become more through our relationship with them. We forget that other students can also grow and learn from the student with AD/HD. So often, the student with AD/HD is emotionally tormented by other students, who are actually being given an opportunity to develop tolerance, compassion, and the unconditional acceptance of others. We have so much to learn from one another. We can learn from the student with AD/HD. Other students can learn from the student with AD/HD. What is it about ourselves that causes us to react the way we do to the child with AD/HD? What is it within us that is threatened and bothered by the carefree spirit of a person different from ourselves? So much of this journey is about ourselves and not our students.

Success is measured by the wealth of a person's experience. Success is a personal judgment. The only person who can truly measure my success is me. We may think that the student with AD/HD is not successful, but we are placing our own value judgment on their experience. Perhaps they experience greater success than we realize. Perhaps they are performing in exactly the way they need to. Perhaps the emotional support and love they receive make the difference. Perhaps loving themselves in spite of the negative messages they receive is part of their life's learning. We cannot measure a person's worth in terms of their academic performance.

We can offer support and opportunities. We can withhold our judgments. We can honor the spirit of the child at all times. If, at the end of the school year, a teacher has done these things, then the teacher will have made a major contribution to the development of the child, regardless of academic achievements.

A student once told me that I was the only teacher who ever understood her. That is how she will always remember me. She may not remember much of the curriculum that I taught. Understanding her was my contribution, my gift, to her. That is what she needed most from me.

As teachers, when we come across that student for whom nothing seems to work, we must continue to implement different strategies and utilize various resources, always remaining positive that something will work. At what point do we give up on a child? Never! Is it sometimes appropriate to consider a change of placement? Absolutely. It may be that a student needs a different environment in order to be successful, but those decisions must be made very carefully and without emotion. Keep in mind that removing a child from an environment in which he has not experienced success will not teach him to be successful in that environment.

10

Advocating for a Student with AD/HD

To be an effective advocate for a student with Attention Deficit/Hyperactivity Disorder, it is imperative that one know the educational, legal, and practical parameters within which we must work.

Much of the information that follows is technical in nature and will require more than one reading. Some may find they do not have a need for all of this information at this time. However, it may become critical at some point in the future. I encourage you to read through this material slowly in order to absorb it adequately. A summary of this information is provided at the end of the chapter.

Educational Parameters

If you have a child with AD/HD who is not experiencing success in the classroom, then you may pursue the appropriate services for your child. Knowing which avenue to pursue can be tough. It is especially difficult for a parent working within a school system that does not seem willing to provide services to students with AD/HD.

In a situation where AD/HD coexists with a learning disability or other qualifying condition under the Individuals with Disabilities Education Act (IDEA), special education is the appropriate avenue to pursue. Typically, there will not be much difficulty in securing services for the student. The AD/HD issues can easily be addressed in the IEP (Individual Education Plan, described later in this chapter). Behavioral goals that address the specific needs of the student should be addressed in the IEP. It is also a good idea to list Other Health Impaired as a qualifying condition in addition to the primary qualifying condition.

For students whose difficulties stem solely from the presence of AD/HD, pursuing accommodations can be much more complex. How does a parent know if a child should qualify under the Individuals with Disabilities Education Act or Section 504 of the ADA (Americans with Disabilities Act)? What type of evaluation should a parent request? These are the first questions to be answered.

It is crucial to remember that a diagnosis of AD/HD does not automatically become a qualifying condition under IDEA or Section 504. What determines the eligibility of a student for services under either category is the impact of the disorder on their performance in a school setting.

The first thing to do is determine the effects within your school setting. How bad are the effects? If the classroom teacher tells you that your child is almost entirely unsuccessful in the classroom, then you can use those reports to assume that the effects are substantial. Once you and the teacher have attempted to work with your child to improve his performance and have not been able to make reasonable improvements, then a referral for special education testing may be necessary. When requesting a special education evaluation, always request the evaluation due to the specific issues present. The teacher and parent reports must indicate, in detail, how the student is unable to perform in the classroom setting and outline the many attempts at intervention that have been made and the results of each attempt.

If a smaller classroom setting with more personalized attention and specialized instruction is what is most appropriate for the child, then special education may be the most appropriate avenue to pursue. It is important to keep in mind that *every* child would benefit from smaller class sizes and more individualized instruction. We must evaluate why we think our child

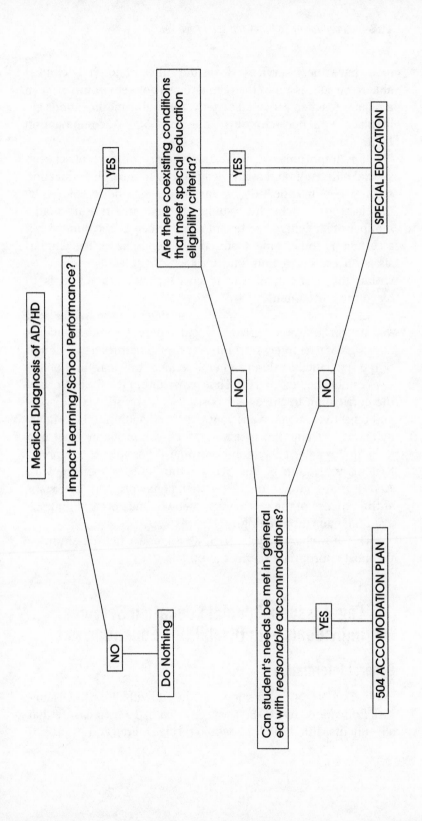

must have these services. If, on the other hand, your child is able to be successful in the regular classroom environment with a regular teacher, provided certain reasonable modifications are in place, you may choose to pursue a 504 Accommodation Plan.

It is important to realize the primary difference between special education and regular education. In a regular education setting, there may be little variance in the methods employed by the classroom teacher from student to student. There are a large number of students to be taught a prescribed curriculum within a certain period of time. Instruction is generalized. The emphasis is on the curriculum and mastery of the skills established within the curriculum. The teacher's primary function is to teach the curriculum.

In contrast, a special education setting offers individualized instruction to a much greater extent. There are fewer students and a greater emphasis on intervention. The primary function of the special education teacher is to meet the goals and objectives established in the IEP. They work within the framework of the curriculum to the extent possible. The priority is the goals and objectives. If you want your child's education to be primarily about learning the curriculum, then you probably want him to be in a regular education classroom if possible. If you prefer that his education be focused on the issues associated with AD/HD (attentional, organizational, behavioral, etc.), perhaps at the expense of the curriculum, then you may prefer to pursue a special education setting.

This flowchart may be used as a guide when determining the most appropriate services to pursue.

Legal Issues: Special Education Services, Individuals with Disabilities Education Act

General Information

Public Law 94-142, also known as the Individuals with Disabilities Education Act (IDEA) was enacted in 1974 to ensure that all students with disabilities would receive a Free and Appropriate Public Education. The law stipulates that for each qualified student, an Individual Education Plan (IEP) must be written within thirty days of the date the student is determined to be eligible. This is a federal mandate for which the states receive federal money to meet the requirements outlined by the law.

In 1997, Congress passed the reauthorization of IDEA. In March 1999, the Department of Education (DOE) published new regulations to implement these changes. These regulations took effect on May 11, 1999. The amendments to IDEA in Public Law 105-17 and the DOE regulations that followed will undoubtedly have an impact on special education services. That impact remains to be seen as local, state, and federal agencies interpret the meaning of the amendments and the new regulations and determine how changes will be made at a state and local level.

The Process

The special education process is initiated with a referral for testing by either school personnel or a parent. After the referral for testing, parents must be notified of the referral and the district must obtain parental consent prior to testing.

To determine eligibility, a student must be evaluated by qualified personnel at no cost to parents. A student may qualify under one or more of thirteen disabling conditions specified in IDEA. Parent and teacher reports, including a medical history, are important components to the evaluation process. Intelligence tests are administered as a part of the evaluation in many states. Performance tests are another key component. The diagnostician or evaluation specialist generates a report that outlines any discrepancy between the student's potential, as measured by the IQ test, and the performance tests given. The actual variance that constitutes a significant discrepancy differs from state to state.

Attention Deficit/Hyperactivity Disorder is not a specified category of eligibility. There is, however, the category Other Health Impaired (OHI), which is appropriate for many students with AD/HD. The OHI category establishes eligibility for a student with a medical condition resulting in limited alertness with an adverse effect on the student's academic performance. The new regulations specify AD/HD as one of several conditions that may fall within this category of eligibility. The legal definition of Other Health Impaired is included in Appendix C. The appropriateness of the Other Health Impaired category must be considered when seeking services for an AD/HD student.

With the evaluation process completed, the school is then required to provide written advance notification of the Multi-Disciplinary Team meeting that will be held to determine eligibility based on the evaluation. A parent may contact the school upon receipt of the notification and request the meeting be rescheduled, if necessary. The committee will consist of the evaluation specialist, an administrator, a special education teacher, a regular education teacher, the parent, and the student. (The regulations specify that parents or school personnel may bring in a consultant to be a member of the IEP team. This section of the regulations can also be found in Appendix C.) Should the committee agree that the student is eligible to receive services, the parent must provide written consent before a student can receive special education services.

If you disagree with the evaluation specialist's findings, you may pursue your right to an independent evaluation. If your request for an independent evaluation is denied, you may pursue the request further through due process. The specific due process information is available from the school and should be given to you at the meeting or upon your request.

Once eligibility is determined, the IEP committee must develop an Individual Education Plan within thirty days. This committee determines the most appropriate placement and modifications for the individual student. An IEP must consist of goals and objectives as well as classroom modifications, ancillary services, and a statement regarding the Least Restrictive Environment for the student's schooling. Individualized goals and objectives are established by the committee to meet the individual needs of the student. All goals should be measurable and are written to address the specific needs of the student.

For most AD/HD students who qualify for special education services, there are behaviors that interfere with school performance. Therefore, I recommend a Functional Behavior Assessment and a Behavior Intervention Plan be included in the IEP for all AD/HD students as a preventative measure. A Functional Behavior Assessment is an assessment of how the student is performing in terms of behavioral appropriateness. It should identify a student's strengths and weaknesses in this area. This assessment drives the Behavior Intervention Plan, which specifically identifies how the student's behavioral weaknesses will be addressed in a positive manner. This assessment is required at certain points during the disciplinary process, though it makes no sense to perform this assessment only after disciplinary issues become problematic.

Classroom modifications are always necessary for students who qualify under IDEA. The IEP establishes what modifications are required for the student. These are written as part of the IEP. Any teacher, including regular education and elective teachers working with the student, is responsible for implementing the modifications.

Goals and objectives are also defined for ancillary services, which include speech and language therapy, adaptive physical education, occupational therapy, and psychological services.

- Speech and language therapy is necessary for students who meet eligibility criteria as Speech and Language Impaired. Depending on the specific needs of the students, they work on semantics, same-and-different concepts, causal relationships, voice issues, and speech issues. Some AD/HD students may receive this service to address an auditory processing deficit.
- Adaptive physical education is available to students with gross motor impairments. These are typically students with severe physical impairments.
- Occupational therapy is available for students with fine motor impairments. This service may be appropriate for the AD/HD student who has significant difficulty with handwriting.

- Psychological services are available to those students with a demonstrated need. The provider will be a licensed social worker, psychologist, school psychologist, or other qualified professional. AD/HD students with anger management issues would benefit from this service as well as those with severe social deficits.

When a student becomes eligible for special education services, under IDEA, many options for program placement become available. It is not always necessary that a qualified student be taken out of the general education classroom. The determination of the Least Restrictive Environment (LRE) is also to be made by the IEP committee. When determining the program, or classroom placement, of a student, the committee must consider a continuum of services. The least restrictive environment available is the general education classroom; it is the same setting as the student's nondisabled peers. The other end of the continuum would be a self-contained classroom consisting of a small number of students (approximately ten or fewer) with one teacher for the entire day. There are levels of restriction between these two extremes. The committee must agree on the least restrictive environment in which this student can receive the services already determined to be necessary to meet his needs and continue to advance in the general curriculum.

When the IEP has been drafted, it is signed by each committee member. One copy remains in the student's file with the special education teacher who is primarily responsible for the implementation of the IEP. Another copy is placed in the student's confidential file, which is a permanent record. One copy is the parent copy.

With an IEP written and services determined, the school system is then obligated to implement the program as established in the IEP. This document requires all school personnel involved with this student to follow the IEP. There is no legal way around it. For as long as the IEP is in place, it is the document that dictates much of how this student is to be educated. The student has specific rights by virtue of the IEP. If, at any time, parents feel that the rights of the student have been violated, they are entitled to due process. The due process procedures must be reviewed with the parents at the IEP meeting and furnished in writing.

The IEP committee must reconvene annually to review and revise the IEP. Every three years, a more extensive review, known as a reevaluation, must be performed.

IDEA Services for Preschool-Age Children

Every state is obligated to identify children with disabilities as young as three years of age. This is known as Child Find. A young child with a diagnosis of AD/HD may be eligible for services through Child Find as Other Health Impaired. Because it can be difficult to obtain a diagnosis of AD/HD for a young child, it is important to find out if your state has a Developmental Delay category. If this category is available, it may be the most appropriate means to securing services for a young child who exhibits the characteristics of AD/HD.

Suspensions and Expulsions

The new regulations sought to address the issue of suspensions and expulsions in a way that was both relevant to our times and maintained protection for all students.

A student who receives special education services may be suspended in accordance with the discipline policies used for all students. There are no restrictions on this for up to ten school days of suspension. When a suspension or series of suspensions results in a change of placement—meaning that the IEP cannot be implemented as written—a review is triggered. When considering suspension, in-school suspension should also be considered. Anytime a student is removed in a manner that prevents him from receiving the services outlined in his IEP, it counts as a suspension. The same is true for the student whose school is sending him home often for misbehaviors, but not completing the paperwork that officially makes it a suspension. This practice should be viewed in the same light as suspensions.

What constitutes a change in placement? A change in placement occurs when a student is suspended for more than ten consecutive school days or when ten or more cumulative days of suspension result in a pattern. What constitutes a pattern? A pattern is established by considering the total number of school days a student is suspended, the length of each removal, and how often a student is being suspended. The special education teacher who is primarily responsible for the implementation of the IEP, other school personnel, or the parent of the student may request an IEP meeting when they suspect a pattern has been established.

Once a review has been triggered, the IEP committee must convene to have a manifestation determination. The manifestation determination poses the following questions:

- Does the student's disability impair his ability to understand the impact and consequences of his behavior?
- Does the student's disability impair his ability to control the behavior?
- In relation to the behavior, was the student's placement appropriate?
- Were the behavior strategies provided for in the IEP being implemented?

If any of the following is determined during the review process, the district is unable to suspend and the IEP must be revised appropriately.

- The student's disability does impair his ability to understand the impact and consequences of his behavior.
- The student's disability does impact his ability to control the behavior.
- The student's placement was not appropriate.
- The behavior strategies provided for by the IEP were not being implemented.

Within ten days of the disciplinary action, the district must perform a functional behavior assessment and develop a behavior intervention plan or review and revise as necessary an existing behavior intervention plan.

For the first ten days of a special education student's suspensions, the district can suspend the student without providing any services. However, beyond ten days of suspension, the district must provide services that enable the student to advance in the general curriculum and make progress toward their IEP goals.

A special education student expelled for a weapons violation or a drug violation automatically triggers a review. The district may expel a student for these violations according to the district's discipline policy. However, the district must provide an interim alternative placement which allows the student to continue to advance and progress.

IDEA 97 also provides protection to students with disabilities who are not yet in the special education system when the school district had a Basis of Knowledge. A Basis of Knowledge exists if the parent has expressed concerns in writing that the student may require special services, there has been a demonstrated need for special services, the parent has requested an evaluation, or school personnel have initiated a process of review or evaluation of the student. The Basis of Knowledge must exist prior to the disciplinary violation. Under these circumstances, the student may be suspended; however, the district must provide an expedited process of evaluation for eligibility. (There is no definition of "expedited" in the statute.)

I have simplified this technical information on the Individuals with Disabilities Education Act as much as possible. However, it is important to realize that there is much more to it than is contained in these few pages. IDEA is an extremely complex law and the reauthorization is still in the early stages of interpretation. The basic information presented here is intended to educate the parents of an AD/HD child about the options that *may* be available and appropriate for their child. It can be used as a basic framework of information and should not be construed as legal advice. Relevant sections of the DOE Regulations are contained in Appendix C.

Legal Issues: Americans with Disabilities Act, Section 504

The Americans with Disabilities Act (ADA) of 1990 defines a person with a disability as:

- A person with a physical or mental impairment that subsequently limits that person in some major life activity (such as walking, talking, breathing, or working)
- A person with a record of a physical or mental impairment
- A person who is regarded as having such an impairment

Certainly, a student with AD/HD could fit into each of these definitions as follows:

- AD/HD is a neurobiological impairment that substantially limits one or more major life activity–specifically learning and/or school performance
- A student with AD/HD will have a record of such impairment
- A student with AD/HD will be regarded as having such impairment

Individuals meeting this definition of disabled are covered under Section 504 of the ADA and they are entitled to accommodations by any public institution, including public schools.

The protection afforded under Section 504 requires that disabled students are to receive an education comparable to their nondisabled peers with reasonable accommodations and an accommodation plan. Section 504 of the ADA is a federal mandate that does not provide the states with any federal money to help meet the needs of students who qualify under this provision.

Evaluations under Section 504 are in great demand. Unfortunately, most school districts are unaware of their obligations or unwilling to perform evaluations under the ADA. They claim it is not their legal responsibility and refer parents to their pediatrician or psychologist. In an Office of Civil Rights (OCR) memorandum published on April 29, 1993 (included in Appendix C), the OCR takes the position that if a parent suspects his child has AD/HD and school personnel also suspect that the student may need special services of some kind, the district is responsible for an appropriate evaluation. If the district refuses to provide for the evaluation, the parent then must be notified of their due process rights. Under due process, a parent can attempt to force the district to provide the evaluation.

For practicality and timing purposes, I recommend that parents have an evaluation performed through their medical provider when possible. I find this to be a much more productive route to take. If you do not have medical insurance, or if your insurance will not cover the cost of an evaluation, then asking the school to provide the evaluation may be your best option, though it may not be the most timely process.

Another issue of great debate in regard to Section 504 is whether or not a student qualified under the ADA is entitled to special education services. Because special education and 504 eligibility are two separate arenas, many districts may be unaware that students eligible under 504 are also eligible to receive special education services. The OCR, in the above-mentioned memorandum, has stated clearly that a student qualified as disabled under the ADA definition is entitled to any appropriate special education services, including ancillary services.

The Process

When a medical diagnosis is in place, you may collect a Physician/Provider Statement, like the one found below, from the current provider.

With this statement in hand, then gather school-related information, such as correspondence, report cards, and disciplinary notices. Then approach the school with a letter explaining how the student meets 504 eligibility based on the diagnosis and the impact the disorder currently has on the student's educational performance. In this letter, we request that a meeting be scheduled to write a 504 Accommodation Plan for the student.

Physician/Health Care Provider Statement

Patient Name _____ Date of Birth _____ Age _____

Physician/Provider _____ Address _____

Phone _____ Fax _____

This is a statement to affirm the diagnosis of Attention Deficit/Hyperactivity Disorder for the aforementioned Patient by the aforementioned Physician/Provider.

Date of evaluation _____ Date of initial diagnosis of AD/HD _____

Please indicate the relevance of each of the following statements:

Yes   No   This patient was first diagnosed as having AD/HD by another physician, and on the date of evaluation listed above, I established my agreement with that diagnosis.

Yes   No   This patient is currently being treated for AD/HD.

Yes   No   The extent of this patient's disorder would be expected to adversely impact his/her educational performance.

Please check each school-related problem that is reasonably anticipated for this patient:

- ☐ lack of concentration
- ☐ difficulty completing assignments
- ☐ difficulty staying seating
- ☐ appearance of lack of motivation
- ☐ easily distracted
- ☐ easily discouraged
- ☐ tendency to rush through assignments
- ☐ Other _____

- ☐ difficulty remaining on task
- ☐ difficulty following directions
- ☐ difficulty getting materials back and forth from home to school, class to class, etc.
- ☐ easily frustrated
- ☐ low test scores
- ☐ frequent interruptions or outbursts

Please check each school-related intervention that may be appropriate for this patient at this time:

- ☐ extended time to complete assignments
- ☐ being allowed to turn in late work
- ☐ individualized behavior management plan
- ☐ modification of homework load
- ☐ Other _____

- ☐ modified assignments
- ☐ assistance with organizational skills
- ☐ preferential seating
- ☐ daily or weekly progress report
- ☐ frequent reminders

Physician/Provider Signature: _____   Date: _____

A 504 Accommodation Plan is written much more simply than an IEP. A committee much like the IEP committee is appropriate. The accommodation plan should include the following elements:

- A complete and accurate description of the nature of the disability
- An explanation of how the disability substantially limits a major life activity
- A description of the reasonable accommodations that are necessary
- A description of how the success of the Accommodation Plan will be measured

I recommend the 504 Accommodation Plan be reviewed initially six months after it is first drafted and then annually after that.

Practical Considerations

In evaluating where a child fits into the legal maze and the educational parameters we must work within, it is also imperative that we be practical. We cannot have the best of both worlds all the time. It is important to realize that schools are institutions and teachers are individuals. There are limitations to what can be accomplished within an institution. There are limits to what can be done by an individual. We must be careful not to expect what is unreasonable or unrealistic.

We must find a balance between what our child is legally entitled to and what is practical. We must know that teachers are not miracle workers and that our child's rights should not interfere with the rights of another child. We must realize that we may not always know how our child reacts and responds in a classroom setting and we must assume that our child will not receive one-on-one attention for much of the school day.

We must thoroughly evaluate what it is we wish to accomplish and how reasonable our requests are. It is always reasonable to ask that a child's needs be addressed in the school setting. It is not always reasonable to dictate how those needs are to be addressed. Many times educators have innovative ways of addressing the needs of students. We have to listen and be open to their suggestions and expertise; only then can we expect that they will listen and be open to ours.

Many times parents want their child to receive special education services without understanding the full ramifications of that environment. For a student who really needs special education, it is often the only way to address their special learning needs. For most students, however, it is not the best alternative. If you have a student who is quite capable of learning grade-level information, it may not be appropriate to put him in a classroom of students three years behind grade level. I often hear parents complain that their child has fallen farther behind since being placed in a special education classroom. This is common for a student who is not appropriately placed. The simple truth is that most students placed in a special education setting are not performing at grade level. It may not be appropriate for a student with AD/HD to be removed from the regular education setting. Also, keep in mind that a parent who wants their child to receive services under IDEA may not be able to secure eligibility as established by the law. Wanting the services will not necessarily mean that your child is legally entitled to them.

In my experience, most students with garden-variety AD/HD can and should be educated in a regular education setting with accommodations and modifications. The most practical way of ensuring that this happens is to initiate a 504 Accommodation Plan.

How to Begin

Knowing your child well, and understanding the nature of the disorder your family lives with is key to this process. Understanding the system is another important preliminary step in becoming a child advocate. The school personnel will know more about the process than you do. However, many teachers and administrators are not yet adequately informed on how to meet the needs of students with AD/HD. They have not always received the information, directives, and tools they need to successfully provide appropriate services for our children. No teacher or administrator knows more about your child than you do. No one else has more insight into your child's world. It is also true that your child performs differently when you are not present. Many parents have a hard time believing this, but it is true. Teachers also bring valuable information about your child to the table. Ultimately, though, a student's success is best facilitated through the collaboration between parents and teachers.

How to proceed initially depends upon whether or not your child has already been diagnosed with AD/HD. If your child does not have a formal diagnosis of AD/HD, I recommend that you pursue an evaluation. There is much to be considered in initiating an evaluation. As discussed in an earlier chapter, you do not want just any doctor performing the evaluation of your child. You want a qualified professional who will do a thorough evaluation.

Preparation for the Meeting

Any parent of an AD/HD child is familiar with the parent-teacher conference and other meetings that are just as uncomfortable and perhaps more intimidating. A meeting to write an IEP or an Accommodation Plan can be overwhelming simply because a parent is outnumbered. Most schools attempt to provide a friendly atmosphere for these meetings, but they can still be stressful events.

To prepare for any school meeting, there are several things a parent can do:

- Gather together all of your notes and paperwork from previous meetings, correspondence, and other relevant documentation. I find it helpful to have a folder with all the information on my child. Review your notes from the previous meeting and spend some time considering how things have been since then. Have you been able to meet the commitments you made? Have the teachers met their commitments? How has your child been doing since the last meeting? Have you seen improvements? Has anything gotten worse? How does your child feel since the last meeting? Write down your thoughts and concerns. Be sure to include positive aspects to share at the meeting.

- Prepare a list of possible strategies, accommodations, and modifications that you would like to see implemented. Understand that ultimately decisions are made as a team. Do not prepare a list of demands.
- Prepare a list of questions you have for the teacher or other school personnel.
- Plan to take someone with you. I feel strongly that the results are better if both parents can attend the meeting. Consider taking a professional advocate with you. You may even want to bring a relative or friend. Having someone with you often decreases your apprehension.
- If you have had a difficult time in the past with someone who will be present at the meeting, prepare yourself mentally not to be triggered emotionally by past events.
- Prepare yourself mentally for the meeting by having a few minutes to quietly center yourself. Take time to be quiet, peaceful, and ready to attend and participate in a beneficial meeting about your child.

At the Meeting

- Be prepared, positive, practical, and open to new ideas and possibilities.
- Do not be pressured into making decisions that you are not comfortable with. You can always state that you are not ready to agree to something today, but that you will return at a later time with your position.
- Do not give in to something you feel is not right in order to avoid a confrontation with the school. If you feel it is not right, you must stand your ground and remember that this is your child.
- If you do not understand something, ask that it be clarified until you do understand.

- If you are not in agreement, and the meeting must end, ask that a continuation be scheduled.

After the Meeting

The job of advocating for a child does not end when the meeting ends. Once you have an IEP or an Accommodation Plan in place, you must remain in contact with the school. There is an individual at the school whose job it is to monitor the implementation of the Plan. Be sure you know who this person is and how to contact him during school hours. It is my strong contention that it is a parent advocate's job to monitor the implementation of the plan. We must make sure the accommodations are provided, and we must monitor our child's progress and commitment, as well.

It is good procedure to follow up with gestures of appreciation when we know that things are being done well for our child. A quick visit to say, "Hello, I think everything is going well, and I'd like to thank you for your work on my daughter's behalf," means a great deal to a teacher. Thank-you notes are also a nice gesture.

When we notice that things are not going so well, or something fell through the cracks, our job is to be on top of that. You may begin with a friendly reminder that you were looking for a report on Friday and did not find it, and a request to have the report sent the following school day, or whatever the case may be. If a friendly reminder is not enough, you may wish to request a telephone conference. It is good to keep a record of any conversations that you have regarding the implementation of your child's plan. If you find it necessary to go beyond a telephone call, you may want to ask for a meeting with the teacher. Follow up on conversations with a written note of confirmation.

I find it absolutely necessary to involve an administrator any time there is a significant conflict with a teacher. The administrator is there to intervene in such a situation. You may not always be fortunate enough to have a helpful administrator to work with, but they must be involved. It often saves vital time and energy.

Is It Just That Easy?

Absolutely not. Anyone who has made a commitment to being a child advocate knows that it is not easy. Sometimes, we are blessed with genuinely wonderful teachers and administrators who will stand on their heads to help our children. Sometimes, our input is welcomed and valued. Sometimes, we are met with resistance and resentment.

When we are faced with a teacher or administrator who is resistant to what we perceive to be the needs of our child, then our job as advocate will not be an easy one. As parents, we cannot help becoming emotional at times. Teachers can also become emotional. When emotions flare, the situation can become worse before it becomes better.

Some school years are easier than others. Regardless of how difficult our task may be, we cannot afford to give up. We must embrace this as the most crucial job we have. Sometimes, we are pioneers in our field. Many parents are intimidated by the school. Many parents feel helpless to change things. We cannot afford to get bogged down in fear and hopelessness. We know that changes can and must be made and we will not give up!

I have wished a hundred times that I had someone to guide me through this process. I cannot express how difficult the journey has been at times. Much of what I have learned, I learned through experience and perseverance.

I have attended many, many school conferences. The most memorable meeting was a situation in which I had received no notes or telephone calls from my son's teacher, so I assumed, foolishly perhaps, that things were going well. At the parent-teacher conference, she discussed with me some problems she was having with Nickolas. Of course, none of these were new to me. I shared with her several strategies that had worked well with Nickolas in the past. I asked her to try them for a couple of weeks and then let me know. About a month later, I had heard nothing from her and I received a Parent Notification of Support Team Meeting. I got the information that I needed and attended the meeting. I listened to this teacher say horrible things about my child. Her problems with my son were affecting her in a profound way. I tried to discuss with her the things that we had learned from past experience with Nickolas. She was not receptive. She said, among other things, that he simply did not care. I reached the end of my emotional rope at this accusation and said to her, "If you cannot find any empathy for my child, then I am sure that not I, nor anyone else in this room, can help you in any way." With that, I left the meeting.

I share this story because I later found that this meeting had an impact on others in the room. The principal later told me that my comment was right on. The teacher did not return to our school the following year. I can only speculate as to the reasons why. Never give up. Always be there 100 percent for your child. Speak the truth. It will set us all free!

Summary

- The first step to advocating for your child with AD/HD is to determine the extent of difficulties being encountered at school. Gather documentation regarding specific elements of his classroom experience.
- The second step is to determine whether or not your child may be eligible for special education services under IDEA, Other Health Impaired. If it is thought that an eligibility may be possible, request a special education evaluation. If it is found that your child does not meet criteria under IDEA, request an Accommodation Plan under Section 504 of the ADA. Often it is a good idea to have a 504 plan implemented while the special education referral is being processed.
- The third step is to develop either an IEP or a 504 Accommodation Plan.
- The fourth, and ongoing, step is to monitor the progress of your child and communicate regularly with school personnel.

11

Where Are We Now?

A s a family, we have grown immeasurably. There is peace in my home today compared to the turbulence of years past. It gets easier as time goes by. We are able to laugh together and work through issues that arise with confidence in ourselves as people who overcome obstacles—one moment at a time. It gets easier because we've made peace with the difficulties and we allow them to be addressed without judgment or shame.

We've made it through Nickolas's first year of high school and Heather's first year of middle school. Both passed all of their classes with a cumulative B average. They each still have their challenges and their hurts. We still encounter all the issues I've addressed in these pages. We face them together though and we don't allow the issues to dominate our lives. My children are happier because they know I believe in them.

As for me, I enjoy being a mom now. I'm no longer under the dark cloud of fear, and what once felt like an immense burden has now become the greatest joy of my life. My role as a mother is a vehicle for my own personal growth. The journey of parenthood is one of genuine love and exquisite joy. I embrace that love and joy each day and am so very grateful for the three beautiful children that I am honored to share my life with. I once asked, "Why me?" but now I know that it had to be me! They are exactly who I need to share my journey with. They are the very people who have helped me to become *me*.

I invite you to honor the spirit of your AD/HD child by

placing your emphasis on the journey. You can be a beneficial presence to your child as you both grow. Dr. Brooks encourages his audience to ask themselves this question: "Is my child a stronger, happier person because of things I have said and done today?" I suggest we ask this of ourselves daily. By making a commitment to conscious parenting, you cannot make a mistake!

===

Diagnostic Criteria for AD/HD

Attention-Deficit/Hyperactivity Disorder: Inattentive Type

Characteristics	Never	Sometimes	Pretty Much	Very Much
Often fails to give close attention to details or makes careless mistakes in schoolwork, work, or other activities.				
Often has difficulty sustaining attention.				
Often does not seem to listen when spoken to directly.				
Often does not follow through on instructions and fails to finish tasks.				
Often has difficulty organizing tasks and activities.				
Often avoids dislikes or is reluctant to engage in tasks that require sustained mental effort (such as schoolwork or homework).				
Often loses things necessary for tasks or activities.				
Is often easily distracted by extraneous stimuli.				
Often is forgetful in daily activities.				

If six or more of these characteristics are rated "pretty much" or "very much," then a diagnosis of *AD/HD: inattentive type* is possible.

Attention Deficit/Hyperactivity Disorder: Hyperactivity/ Impulsive Type

Characteristics	Never	Sometimes	Pretty Much	Very Much
Often fidgets with hands or feet or squirms in seat.				
Often leaves seat in classroom or other situations.				
Often runs about or climbs excessively (in adolescents or adults, may be limited to subjective feelings of restlessness).				
Often has difficulty doing things quietly.				
Is often "on the go" or acts as if "driven by a motor."				
Often talks excessively.				
Often blurts out answers before the questions are completed.				
Often has difficulty awaiting turn.				
Often interrupts or intrudes on others.				

If six of these characteristics are rated as "pretty much" or "very much," then a diagnosis of *AD/HD: hyperactive/impulsive type* is possible.

Attention Deficit/Hyperactivity Disorder: Combined Type

If the criteria for AD/HD: inattentive type and the criteria for AD/HD hyperactive/impulsive type are met, then a diagnosis of AD/HD: combined type is possible.

Other Criteria for Diagnosis of Attention Deficit/ Hyperactivity Disorder

Criteria	Yes	No
Some hyperactive/impulsive or inattentive symptoms that caused impairment present before age 7.		
Some impairment from the symptoms present in two or more settings (e.g. school and home).		
Clear evidence of clinically significant impairment in social, academic, or occupational functioning.		
Symptoms did not occur exclusively during the course of a pervasive developmental disorder, schizophrenia, or other psychotic disorder, and are not better accounted for by another mental disorder (e.g. mood disorder, anxiety disorder).		

Attention Deficit/Hyperactivity Disorder: Not Otherwise Specified

This category has been established by the *Diagnostic Statistical Manual* for those with prominent symptoms of inattention or hyperactivity/impulsivity that do not meet criteria for attention-deficit/hyperactivity disorder.

Oppositional Defiant Disorder

Characteristics	Never	Sometimes	Pretty Much	Very Much
Often loses temper.				
Often argues with adults.				
Often actively denies or refuses to comply with adults' requests or rules.				
Often deliberately annoys people.				
Often blames others for his or her mistakes or misbehaviors.				
Is often touchy or easily annoyed by others.				
Is often angry and resentful.				
Is often spiteful or vindictive.				

If four or more of these characteristics have been present for six months or longer, then a diagnosis of *oppositional defiant disorder* is possible.

Other Criteria for Oppositional Defiant Disorder

Criteria	Yes	No
The disturbance in behavior causes clinically significant impairment in social, academic, or occupational functioning.		
Behaviors do not occur exclusively during the course of a psychotic or mood disorder.		
Criteria are not met for conduct disorder and, if 18 years or older, antisocial personality disorder.		

Behavior Goals	Monday	Tuesday	Wednesday	Thursday	Friday

This report can be modified to be used as a daily report as well as weekly. Behaviors being reinforced are listed in the far left column and boxes can simply be initialed or checked off as appropriate. This report is best used with young children. Stickers work well in the boxes; the absence of a sticker indicates the goal was not met.

Daily Progress Report

Student Name: _____ Day: _____ Date: _____

Period: _____ Class: _____ Subject: _____ Teacher: _____

Attitude	Excellent	Acceptable	Unacceptable (see reverse)
On-task behavior	Excellent	Acceptable	Unacceptable (see reverse)
Productivity	Excellent	Acceptable	Unacceptable (see reverse)
Assignments due today turned in		Yes	No (see reverse)
Homework assigned		Yes	No
Estimated Grade Average	A/B	C	D/F

Period: _____ Class: _____ Subject: _____ Teacher: _____

Attitude	Excellent	Acceptable	Unacceptable (see reverse)
On-task behavior	Excellent	Acceptable	Unacceptable (see reverse)
Productivity	Excellent	Acceptable	Unacceptable (see reverse)
Assignments due today turned in		Yes	No (see reverse)
Homework assigned		Yes	No
Estimated Grade Average	A/B	C	D/F

Period: _____ Class: _____ Subject: _____ Teacher: _____

Attitude	Excellent	Acceptable	Unacceptable (see reverse)
On-task behavior	Excellent	Acceptable	Unacceptable (see reverse)
Productivity	Excellent	Acceptable	Unacceptable (see reverse)
Assignments due today turned in		Yes	No (see reverse)
Homework assigned		Yes	No
Estimated Grade Average	A/B	C	D/F

Period: _____ Class: _____ Subject: _____ Teacher: _____

Attitude	Excellent	Acceptable	Unacceptable (see reverse)
On-task behavior	Excellent	Acceptable	Unacceptable (see reverse)
Productivity	Excellent	Acceptable	Unacceptable (see reverse)
Assignments due today turned in		Yes	No (see reverse)
Homework assigned		Yes	No
Estimated Grade Average	A/B	C	D/F

Period: _____ Class: _____ Subject: _____ Teacher: _____

Attitude	Excellent	Acceptable	Unacceptable (see reverse)
On-task behavior	Excellent	Acceptable	Unacceptable (see reverse)
Productivity	Excellent	Acceptable	Unacceptable (see reverse)
Assignments due today turned in		Yes	No (see reverse)
Homework assigned		Yes	No
Estimated Grade Average	A/B	C	D/F

Period: _____ Class: _____ Subject: _____ Teacher: _____

Attitude	Excellent	Acceptable	Unacceptable (see reverse)
On-task behavior	Excellent	Acceptable	Unacceptable (see reverse)
Productivity	Excellent	Acceptable	Unacceptable (see reverse)
Assignments due today turned in		Yes	No (see reverse)
Homework assigned		Yes	No
Estimated Grade Average	A/B	C	D/F

Parent Signature: (comments on reverse) _____

Classroom Strategies for Teachers

Self-Concept Issues
> Praise student regularly.
> Emphasize positive qualities of the student.
> Provide opportunities to demonstrate strengths.
> Facilitate transition of negative traits to positive traits (e.g., changing bossiness to leadership).
> Honor student's accomplishments publicly.
> Decrease demands not being met.
> Avoid public reprimands.

Environmental Issues
> Involve student in seating chart decisions.
> Seat near critical areas (e.g. assignment board, pencil sharpener).
> Seat away from areas of auditory distraction.
> Provide stimulating environment.
> Establish climate of acceptance, free from ridicule.
> Provide structured, consistent environment. Label critical areas.
> Display classroom rules.
> Display daily schedule.

Behavior Issues

Identify expectations in advance.

State expectations in terms of specific behaviors.

Do not attempt to limit physical activity.

Provide student with opportunities to channel physical activity.

Provide student pipe cleaners to fidget with.

Provide warnings prior to transitions.

Send student on errands when obviously restless.

Allow student to sit awkwardly in seat or stand to work.

Reward student for raising hand without speaking.

Make regular eye contact with student.

Direct student what to do instead of what not to do.

Limit student's input during discussion with comment coupons, if necessary.

Establish behavior goals (limit the number of goals to 3).

Prioritize/pick your battles.

Develop consequences and rewards in advance.

Develop consequences with a set beginning and end.

Respond calmly to misbehavior.

Do not engage in dialogue about established consequences.

Deliver consequences in a matter-of-fact manner.

Implement self-management program.

Implement use of behavior chart or checklist.

Observe student frequently.

Provide specific, positive, immediate feedback.

Involve parents in monitoring progress.

Provide warnings prior to disciplinary action.

Allow for restitution.

Provide positive and frequent reinforcement.

Be consistent.

Praise improvement. Reward improvement.

Avoid discussion of past infractions.

Social Issues

Reinforce social cues.

Emphasize social routines.

Group with nonjudgmental peers.

Model behaviors when appropriate.

Avoid public corrections.
Implement behavior contract.
Focus on 1 to 2 social goals at a time.

Organizational Issues

Allow class time to organize notebooks, clean desks, etc.
Provide frequent organizational cues and reminders.
Establish routines.
Display daily and homework assignments in one place.
Implement color coding.
Implement system of labeling.
Simplify student's organizational system.
Monitor use of planner/assignment chart. Allow tape recording of lectures for later note-taking instruction.
Allow students to share notes.
Provide a structured note-taking format.
Review notes with student.

Task Completion Issues

Solicit student input.
Present material in a novel way.
Allow student to work on more than one assignment simultaneously/shift focus back and forth.
Provide choices for assignments.
Avoid monotonous tasks.
Intersperse high-interest tasks with low-interest tasks.
Provide several small practice activities instead of one large practice assignment.
Break tasks down into manageable chunks.
Implement the use of a timer.
Establish cues for off-task behavior.
Reinforce improvement.
Implement visuals for assignments/overhead when lecturing.
Allow frequent breaks.
Modify assignments with fewer problems/items to be completed.
Extend time allowed to complete tasks. Allow doodling.
Provide constant feedback regarding student's progress.

Set short-term goals for completion of smaller units.
Avoid sending incomplete assignments home.
Limit amount of homework/modify homework assignments.
Review student progress regularly.
Have student repeat instructions.
Allow use of typewriter, computer, etc.
Provide some assignments on colored paper.
Alternate activities.
Use teaching games frequently.

Evaluation Issues

Provide advance opportunities for in-class studying/reviewing.
Provide pretest opportunities.
Modify amount of material to be tested on.
Monitor student progress during testing.
Develop clear, legible, uncluttered test forms.
Highlight key words and phrases and review orally with student.
Allow for additional time to complete testing.
Allow for short breaks during testing.
Review entire test with student prior to beginning.
Have student read directions orally before beginning.
Review test with student before handing it in for incompleteness or obvious errors and omissions.
Allow credit for corrections.

Appendix **C**

Legal Reference

Individuals with Disabilities Education Act Statutes

The following statutes are from the Department of Education Regulations that are based on the 1997 reauthorization of the Individuals with Disabilities Education Act, Public Law 105-17. These regulations were effective as of May 11, 1999. The regulations, in their entirety, are available as public information by contacting the U.S. Department of Education. They are also available via the Internet. The following statutes are especially important for students with Attention Deficit/Hyperactivity Disorder.

AD/HD and IDEA Eligibility

Subpart A; Section 300.7

(9) Other Health Impairment means having limited strength, vitality or alertness, including a heightened alertness to environmental stimuli, that results in limited alertness with respect to the educational environment, that—

(i) Is due to chronic or acute health problems such as asthma, attention deficit disorder or attention deficit hyperactivity disorder, diabetes, epilepsy, a heart condition, hemophilia, lead poisoning, leukemia, nephritis, rheumatic fever, and sickle cell anemia; and

(ii) Adversely affects a child's educational performance.

Three- and Four-Year-Old Children

Subpart A; Section 300.7   Child with a Disability.

(b) Children aged 3 through 9 experiencing developmental delays. The term child with a disability for children aged 3 through 9 may, at the discretion of the State and LEA and in accordance with Section 300.313, include a child—

(1) Who is experiencing developmental delays, as defined by the State and as measured by appropriate diagnostic instruments and procedures, in one or more of the following areas; physical development, cognitive development, communication development, social or emotional development, or adaptive development; and

(2) Who, by reason thereof, needs special education and related services.

Subpart B; Section 300.121   Free appropriate public education (FAPE).

(c) FAPE for children beginning at age 3. (1) Each State shall ensure that—

(i) The obligation to make FAPE available to each eligible child residing in the State begins no later than the child's third birthday; and

(ii) An IEP or IFSP is in effect for the child by that date, in accordance with Section 300.342 (c).

(2) If a child's third birthday occurs during the summer, the child's IEP team shall determine the date when services under the IEP or IFSP will begin.

Subpart C; Section 300.300   Provision of FAPE.

(a) General. (1) Subject to paragraphs (b) and (c) of this section and Section 300.311, each State receiving assistance under this part shall ensure that FAPE is available to all children with disabilities, aged 3 through 21, residing in the State including children with disabilities who have been suspended or expelled from school.

(2) As a part of its obligation under paragraph (a) (1) of this section, each State must ensure that the requirements of Section 300.125 (to identify, locate, and evaluate all children with disabilities) are implemented by public agencies throughout the State.

(3) (i) The services provided to the child under this part address all of the child's identified special education and related services needs described in paragraph (a) of this section.

(ii) The services and placement needed by each child with a disability to receive FAPE must be based on the child's unique needs and not on the child's disability.

Subpart C; Section 300.313   Children Experiencing Developmental Delays.

(a) Use of term developmental delay. (1) A state that adopts the term developmental delay under Section 300.7 (b) determines whether it applies to children aged 3 through 9, or to a subset of that age range (e.g., ages 3 through 5).

(2) A State may not require an LEA to adopt and use the term developmental delay for any children within its jurisdiction.

(3) If an LEA uses the term developmental delay for children described in Section 300.7 (b), the LEA must conform to both the State's definition of that term and to the age range that has been adopted by the State.

(4) If a state does not adopt the term developmental delay, an LEA may not independently use that term as a basis for establishing a child's eligibility under this part.

(b) Use of individual disability categories. (1) Any State or LEA that elects to use the term developmental delay for children aged 3 through 9 may also use one or more of the disability categories described in Section 300.7 for any child within that age range if it is determined, through the evaluation conducted under Section 300.530–300.536, that the child has an impairment described in Section 300.7, and because of that impairment needs special education and related services.

(2) The state or LEA shall ensure that all of the child's special education and related services needs that have been identified through the evaluation described in paragraph (b) (1) of this section are appropriately addressed.

Individual Education Programs

Subpart C; Section 300.342   When IEPs must be in effect.

(d) Effective date for new requirements. All IEPs developed, reviewed, or revised on or after July 1, 1998 must meet the requirements of Sections 300.340–300.350.

Subpart C; Section 300.343   IEP meetings.

(a) General. Each public agency is responsible for initiating and conducting meetings for the purpose of developing, reviewing, and revising the IEP of a child with a disability (or, if consistent with Section 300.342 (c), an IFSP).

(b) Initial IEPs; provision of services.

(1) Each public agency shall ensure that within a reasonable period of time following the agency's receipt of parent consent to an initial evaluation of a child—

(i) The child is evaluated; and

(ii) If determined eligible under this part, special education and related services are made available to the child in accordance with an IEP.

(2) In meeting the requirements in paragraph (b) (1) of this section, a meeting to develop an IEP for the child must be conducted within 30 days of a determination that the child needs special education and related services.

(c) Review and revision of the IEPs. Each public agency shall ensure that the IEP team—

(1) Reviews the child's IEP periodically, but not less than annually, to determine whether the annual goals for the child are being achieved; and

(2) Revises the IEP as appropriate to address—

(i) Any lack of expected progress toward the annual goals described in Section 300.347 (a), and in the general curriculum, if appropriate;

(ii) The results of any reevaluation conducted under Section 300.536;

(iii) Information about the child provided to, or by, the parents, as described in Section 300.533 (a) (1);

(iv) The child's anticipated needs; or

(v) Other matters.

Subpart C; Section 300.344   IEP team.

(a) General. The public agency shall ensure that the IEP team for each child with a disability includes—

(1) The parents of the child;

(2) At least one regular education teacher of the child (if the

child is, or may be, participating in the regular education environment);

(3) At least one special education teacher of the child, or if appropriate, at least one special education provider of the child;

(4) A representative of the public agency who

(i) Is qualified to provide, or supervise the provision of, specially designed instruction to meet the unique needs of children with disabilities;

(ii) Is knowledgeable about the general curriculum; and

(iii) Is knowledgeable about the availability of resources of the public agency;

(5) An individual who can interpret the instructional implications of evaluation results, who may be a member of the team described in paragraphs (a) (2) through (6) of this section;

(6) At the discretion of the parent or the agency, other individuals who have knowledge or special expertise regarding the child, including related services personnel as appropriate; and

(7) If appropriate, the child.

(b) Transition services participants. (1) Under paragraph (a) (7) of this section, the public agency shall invite a student with a disability of any age to attend his or her IEP meeting if a purpose of the meeting will be the consideration of–

(i) The student's transition services needs under Section 300.347 (b) (1);

(ii) The needed transition services for the student under Section 300.347 (b) (2); or

(iii) Both.

(2) If the student does not attend the IEP meeting, the public agency shall take other steps to ensure that the student's preferences and interests are considered.

(3) (i) In implementing the requirements of Section 300.347 (b) (2), the public agency also shall invite a representative of any other agency that is likely to be responsible for providing or paying for transition services.

(ii) If an agency invited to send a representative to a meeting does not do so, the public agency shall take other steps to obtain participation of the other agency in the planning of any transition services.

(c) Determination of knowledge and special expertise. The

determination of the knowledge or special expertise of any individual described in paragraph (a) (6) of this section shall be made by the party (parents or public agency) who invited the individual to be a member of the IEP.

(d) Designating a public agency representative. A public agency may designate another public agency member of the IEP team to also serve as the agency representative, if the criteria in paragraph (a) (4) of this section are satisfied.

Subpart C; Section 300.345   Parent participation.

(a) Public agency responsibility–general. Each public agency shall take steps to ensure that one or both of the parents of a child with a disability are present at each IEP meeting or are afforded the opportunity to participate, including–

(1) Notifying parents of the meeting early enough to ensure that they will have an opportunity to attend; and

(2) Scheduling the meeting at a mutually agreed on time and place.

(b) Information provided to parents. (1) The notice required under paragraph (a) (1) of this section must–

(i) Indicate the purpose, time, and location of the meeting and who will be in attendance; and

(ii) Inform the parents of the provisions in Section 300.344 (a) (6) and (c) (relating to the participation of other individuals on the IEP team who have knowledge or special expertise about the child).

(2) For a student with a disability beginning at age 14, or younger, if appropriate, the notice must also–

(i) Indicate that a purpose of the meeting will be the development of a statement of the transition services needs of the student required in Section 300.347 (b) (1); and

(ii) Indicate that the agency will invite the student.

(3) For a student with a disability beginning at age 16, or younger, if appropriate, the notice must–

(i) Indicate that a purpose of the meeting is the consideration of needed transition services for the student required in Section 300.347 (b) (2);

(ii) Indicate that the agency will invite the student; and

(iii) Identify any other agency that will be invited to send a representative.

(c) Other methods to ensure parent participation. If neither parent can attend, the public agency shall use other methods to ensure parent participation, including individual or conference telephone calls.

(d) Conducting an IEP meeting without a parent in attendance. A meeting may be conducted without a parent in attendance if the public agency is unable to convince the parents that they should attend. In this case the public agency must have a record of its attempts to arrange a mutually agreed on time and place, such as—

(1) Detailed records of telephone calls made or attempted and the results of those calls;

(2) Copies of correspondence sent to the parents and any responses received; and

(3) Detailed records of visits made to the parent's home or place of employment and the results of those visits.

(e) Use of interpreters or other action, as appropriate. The public agency shall take whatever action is necessary to ensure that the parent understand the proceedings at the IEP meeting, including arranging for an interpreter for parents with deafness or whose native language is other than English.

(f) Parent copy of child's IEP. The public agency shall give the parent a copy of the child's IEP at no cost to the parent.

Subpart C; Section 300.346   Development, review, and revision of IEP.

(a) Development of IEP. (1) General. In developing each child's IEP, the IEP team, shall consider—

(i) The strengths of the child and the concerns of the parents for enhancing the education of their child;

(ii) The results of the initial or most recent evaluation of the child; and

(iii) As appropriate, the results of the child's performance on any general State or district-wide assessment programs.

(2) Consideration of special factors. The IEP team also shall—

(i) In the case of a child whose behavior impedes his or her learning or that of others, consider, if appropriate, strategies, including positive behavioral interventions, strategies, and supports to address that behavior;

(b) Review and revision of IEP. In conducting a meeting to review, and, if appropriate, revise a child's IEP, the IEP team shall consider the factors described in paragraph (a) of this section.

(c) Statement in IEP. If, in considering the special factors described in paragraphs (a) (1) and (2) of this section, the IEP team determines that a child needs a particular device or service (including an intervention, accommodation, or other program modification) in order for the child to receive FAPE, the IEP team must include a statement to that effect in the child's IEP.

(d) Requirement with respect to regular education teacher. The regular education teacher of a child with a disability, as a member of the IEP team, must, to the extent appropriate, participate in the development, review, and revision of the child's IEP, including assisting in the determination of—

(1) Appropriate positive behavioral interventions and strategies for the child; and

(2) Supplementary aids and services, program modifications or supports for school personnel that will be provided for the child, consistent with Section 300.347 (a) (3).

(e) Construction. Nothing in this section shall be construed to require the IEP team to include information under one component of a child's IEP that is already contained under another component of the child's IEP.

Subpart C; Section 300.347   Content of the IEP.

(a) General. The IEP for each child with a disability must include—

(1) A statement of the child's present levels of educational performance, including—

(i) How the child's disability affects the child's involvement and progress in the general curriculum (i.e., the same curriculum as for nondisabled children); or

(ii) For preschool children, as appropriate, how the disability affects the child's participation in appropriate activities;

(2) A statement of measurable annual goals, including benchmarks or short-term objectives, related to—

(i) Meeting the child's needs that result from the child's disability to enable the child to be involved in and progress in the general curriculum (i.e., the same curriculum as for nondisabled children), or for preschool children, as appropriate, to participate in appropriate activities; and

(ii) Meeting each of the child's other educational needs that result from the child's disability;

(3) A statement of the special education and related services and supplementary aids and services to be provided to the child, or on behalf of the child, and a statement of the program modifications or supports for school personnel that will be provided for the child—

(i) To advance appropriately toward attaining the annual goals;

(ii) To be involved and progress in the general curriculum in accordance with paragraph (a) (1) of this section and to participate in extracurricular and other nonacademic activities; and

(iii) To be educated and participate with other children with disabilities and nondisabled children in the activities described in this section;

(4) An explanation of the extent, if any, to which the child will not participate with nondisabled children in the regular class and in the activities described in paragraph (a) (3) of this section;

(5) (i) A statement of any individual modifications in the administration of State or district-wide assessments of student achievement that are needed in order for the child to participate in the assessment; and

(ii) If the IEP team determines that the child will not participate in a particular State or district-wide assessment of student achievement (or part of an assessment), a statement of—

(A) Why that assessment is not appropriate for the child; and

(B) How the child will be assessed;

(6) The projected date for the beginning of the services and modifications described in paragraph (a) (3) of this section, and the anticipated frequency, location, and duration of those services and modifications; and

(7) A statement of—

(i) How the child's progress toward the annual goals described in paragraph (a) (2) of this section will be measured; and

(ii) How the child's parents will be regularly informed (through such means as periodic report cards), at least as often as parents are informed of their nondisabled children's progress, of–

(A) Their child's progress toward the annual goals; and

(B) The extent to which that progress is sufficient to enable the child to achieve the goals by the end of the year.

(b) Transition services. The IEP must include–

(1) For each student with a disability beginning at age 14 (or younger, if determined appropriate by the IEP team), and updated annually, a statement of the transition service needs of the student under the applicable components of the student's IEP that focuses on the student's courses of study (such as participation in advanced-placement courses or a vocational education program); and

(2) For each student beginning at age 16 (or younger, if determined appropriate by the IEP team), a statement of needed transition services for the student, including, if appropriate, a statement of the interagency responsibilities or any needed linkages.

(c) Transfer of rights. In a State that transfers rights at the age majority, beginning at least one year before a student reaches the age of majority under State law, the student's IEP must include a statement that the student has been informed of his or her rights under Part B of the Act, if any, that will transfer to the student on reaching the age of majority, consistent with Section 300.517.

Subpart C; Section 300.350   IEP-accountability.

(a) Provision of services. Subject to paragraph (b) of this section, each public agency must–

(1) Provide special education and related services to a child with a disability in accordance with the child's IEP; and

(2) Make a good faith effort to assist the child to achieve the goals and objectives or benchmarks listed in the IEP.

(b) Accountability. Part B of the Act does not require that any agency, teacher, or other person be held accountable if a child does not achieve the growth projected in the annual goals and benchmarks or objectives. However, the Act does not prohibit a State or public agency from establishing its own accountability systems regarding teacher, school, or agency performance.

(c) Construction—parent rights. Nothing in this section limits a parent's right to ask for revisions of the child's IEP or to invoke due process procedures if the parent feels that the efforts required in paragraph (a) of this section are not being made.

Suspensions and Expulsions

Subpart B; Section 300.121   Free appropriate public education (FAPE).

(d) FAPE for children suspended or expelled from school. (1) A public agency need not provide services during periods of removal under Section 300.520 (a) (1) to a child with a disability who has been removed from his or her current placement for 10 school days or less in that school year, if services are not provided to a child without disabilities who has been similarly removed.

(2) In the case of a child with a disability who has been removed from his or her current placement for more than 10 school days in that school year, the public agency, for the remainder of the removals, must—

(i) Provide services to the extent necessary to enable the child to appropriately progress in the general curriculum and appropriately advance toward achieving the goals set out in the child's IEP, if the removal is—

(A) Under the school personnel's authority to remove for not more than 10 consecutive school days as long as that removal does not constitute a change of placement under Section 300.519 (b) (Section 300.520 ((a) (1)); or

(B) For behavior that is not a manifestation of the child's disability, consistent with Section 300.524; and

(ii) Provide services consistent with Section 300.522 regarding determination of the appropriate interim alternative educational setting, if the removal is—

(A) For drug or weapons offenses under Section 300.520 (a) (2); or

(B) Based on a hearing officer's determination that maintaining the current placement of the child is substantially likely to result in injury to the child or to others if he or she remains in the current placement consistent with Section 300.521.

(3) (i) School personnel, in consultation with the child's special education teacher, determine the extent to which services are necessary to enable the child to appropriately progress in the general curriculum and appropriately advance toward achieving the goals set out in the child's IEP if the child is removed under the authority of school personnel to remove for not more than 10 consecutive school days as long as that removal does not constitute a change of placement under Section 300.519 (Section 300.520 (a) (1)).

(ii) The child's IEP team determines the extent to which services are necessary to enable the child to appropriately progress in the general curriculum and appropriately advance toward achieving the goals set out in the child's IEP if the child is removed because of behavior that has been determined not to be a manifestation of the child's disability, consistent with Section 300.524.

Subpart E; Section 300.519   Change of placement for disciplinary removals.

For purposes of removals of a child with a disability from the child's current educational placement under Sections 300.520–300.529, a change of placement occurs if–

(a) The removal is for more than 10 consecutive school days; or

(b) The child is subjected to a series of removals that constitute a pattern because they cumulate to more than 10 school days in a school year, and because of factors such as the length of each removal, the total amount of time the child is removed, and the proximity of the removals to one another.

Section 300.520   Authority of school personnel.

(a) School personnel may order–

(1) (i) To the extent removal would be applied to children without disabilities, the removal of a child with a disability from the child's current placement for not more than 10 consecutive school days for any violation of school rules, and additional removals of not more than 10 consecutive school days in that same school year for separate incidents of misconduct (as long

as those removals do not constitute a change of placement under Section 300.519 (b));

(ii) After a child with a disability has been removed from his or her current placement for more than 10 school days in the same school year, during any subsequent days of removal the public agency must provide services to the extent required under Section 300.121 (d); and

(2) A change in placement of a child with a disability to an appropriate interim alternative educational setting for the same amount of time that a child without a disability would be subject to discipline, but for not more than 45 days if—

(i) The child carries or possesses a weapon to or at school or to a school function under the jurisdiction of State or a local educational agency; or

(ii) The child knowingly possesses or uses illegal drugs or sells or solicits the sale of a controlled substance while at school or a school function under the jurisdiction of a State or local educational agency.

(b) (1) Either before or not later than 10 business days after either first removing the child for more than 10 school days in a school year or commencing a removal that constitutes a change of placement under Section 300.519, including the action described in paragraph (a) (2) of this section—

(i) If the LEA did not conduct a functional behavioral assessment and implement a behavioral intervention plan for the child before the behavior that resulted in the removal described in paragraph (a) of this section, the agency shall convene an IEP meeting to develop an assessment plan.

(ii) If the child already has a behavioral intervention plan, the IEP team shall meet to review the plan and its implementation, and modify the plan and its implementation as necessary, to address the behavior.

(2) As soon as practicable after developing the plan described in paragraph (b) (1) (i) of this section, and completing the assessments required by the plan, the LEA shall convene an IEP meeting to develop appropriate behavioral interventions to address that behavior and shall implement those interventions.

(c) (1) If subsequently, a child with a disability who has a behavioral intervention plan and who has been removed from the child's current educational placement for more than 10 school days in a school year is subjected to a removal that does not constitute a change of placement under Section 300.519, the IEP team members shall review the behavioral intervention plan and its implementation to determine if modifications are necessary.

(2) If one or more of the team members believe that modifications are needed, the team shall meet to modify the plan and its implementation, to the extent the team determines necessary.

Subpart E; Section 300.522   Determination of setting.

(a) General. The interim alternative educational setting referred to in Section 300.520 (a) (2) must be determined by the IEP team.

(b) Additional requirements. Any interim alternative educational setting in which a child is placed under Sections 300.520 (a) (2) or 300.521, must—

(1) Be selected so as to enable the child to continue to progress in the general curriculum, although in another setting, and to continue to receive those services and modifications, including those described in the child's current IEP, that will enable the child to meet the goals set out in that IEP; and

(2) Include services and modifications to address the behavior described in Sections 300.520 (a) (2) or 300.521, that are designed to prevent the behavior from recurring.

Subpart E; Section 300.523   Manifestation determination review.

(a) General. If an action is contemplated regarding behavior described in Sections 300.520 (a) (2) or 300.521, or involving a removal that constitutes a change of placement under Section 300.519 for a child with a disability who has engaged in other behavior that violated any rule or code of conduct of the LEA that applies to all children—

(1) Not later than the date on which the decision to take that action is made, the parents must be notified of that decision and provided the procedural safeguards notice described in Section 300.504; and

(2) Immediately, if possible, but in no case later than 10 school days after the date on which the decision to take that ac-

tion is made, a review must be conducted of the relationship between the child's disability and the behavior subject to the disciplinary action.

(b) Individuals to carry out review. A review described in paragraph (a) of this section must be conducted by the IEP team and other qualified personnel in a meeting.

(c) Conduct of review. In carrying out a review described in paragraph (a) of this section, the IEP team and other qualified personnel may determine that the behavior of the child was not a manifestation of the child's disability only if the IEP team and other qualified personnel—

(1) First consider, in terms of the behavior subject to disciplinary action, all relevant information, including—

(i) Evaluation and diagnostic results, including the results or other relevant information supplied by the parents of the child;

(ii) Observations of the child; and

(iii) The child's IEP and placement; and

(2) Then determine that—

(i) In relationship to the behavior subject to disciplinary action, the child's IEP and placement were appropriate and the special education services, supplementary aids and services, and behavior intervention strategies were provided consistent with the child's IEP and placement;

(ii) The child's disability did not impair the ability of the child to understand the impact and consequences of the behavior subject to disciplinary action; and

(iii) The child's disability did not impair the ability of the child to control the behavior subject to disciplinary action.

(d) Decision. If the IEP team and other qualified personnel determine that any of the standards in paragraph (c) (2) of this section were not met, the behavior must be considered a manifestation of the child's disability.

(e) Meeting. The review described in paragraph (a) of this section may be conducted at the same IEP meeting that is convened under Section 300.520 (b).

(f) Deficiencies in IEP or placement. If, in the review in paragraphs (b) and (c) of this section, a public agency identified deficiencies in the child's IEP or placement or in their implementation, it must take immediate steps to remedy those deficiencies.

Subpart E. Section 300.524   Determination that behavior was not a manifestation of disability.

(a) General. If the result of the review described in Section 300.523 is a determination, consistent with Section 300.523 (d), that the behavior of the child with a disability was not a manifestation of the child's disability, the relevant disciplinary procedures applicable to children without disabilities may be applied to the child in the same manner in which they would be applied to children without disabilities, except as provided in Section 300.121 (d).

Children Not Yet Eligible

Subpart E; Section 300.527   Protections for children not yet eligible for special education and related services.

(a) General. A child who has not been determined to be eligible for special education and related services under this part and who has engaged in behavior that violated any rule or code of conduct of the local educational agency, including any behavior described in Sections 300.520 or 300.521, may assert any of the protections provided for in this part if the LEA had knowledge (as determined in accordance with paragraph (b) of this section) that the child was a child with a disability before the behavior that precipitated the disciplinary action occurred.

(b) Basis of knowledge. An LEA must be deemed to have knowledge that a child is a child with a disability if–

(1) The parent of the child has expressed concern in writing (or orally if the parent does not know how to write or has a disability that prevents a written statement) to personnel of the appropriate educational agency that the child is in need of special education and related services;

(2) The behavior or performance of the child demonstrates the need for these services, in accordance with Section 300.7;

(3) The parent of the child has requested an evaluation of the child pursuant to Sections 300.530–300.536; or

(4) The teacher of the child, or other personnel of the local educational agency, has expressed concern about the behavior or performance of the child to the director of special education of the agency or to other personnel in accordance with the agency's established Child Find or special education referral system.

(c) Exception. A public agency would not be deemed to have knowledge under paragraph (b) of this section if, as a result of receiving the information specified in that paragraph, the agency—

(1) Either—

(i) Conducted an evaluation under Sections 300.530–300.536, and determined that the child was not a child with a disability under this part; or

(ii) Determined that an evaluation was not necessary; and

(2) Provided notice to the child's parents of its determination under paragraph (c) (1) of this section consistent with Section 300.503.

(d) Conditions that apply if no basis of knowledge.

(1) General. If an LEA does not have knowledge that a child is a child with a disability (in accordance with paragraphs (b) and (c) of this section) prior to taking disciplinary measures against the child, the child may be subjected to the same disciplinary measures applied to children without disabilities who engage in comparable behaviors consistent with paragraph (d) (2) of this section.

(2) Limitations. (i) If a request is made for an evaluation of a child during the time period in which the child is subjected to disciplinary measures under Section 300.520 or 300.521, the evaluation must be conducted in an expedited manner.

(ii) Until the evaluation is completed, the child remains in the educational placement determined by school authorities, which can include suspension or expulsion without educational services.

(iii) If the child is determined to be a child with a disability, taking into consideration information from the evaluation conducted by the agency and information provided by the parents, the agency shall provide special education and related services in accordance with the provisions of this part, including the requirements of Section 300.520–300.529 and section 612 (a) (1) (A) of the Act.

Procedural Safeguards

Subpart E; Section 300.503   Prior Notice by the public agency; content of notice.

(a) Notice. (1) Written notice that meets the requirements of paragraph (b) of this section must be given to the parents of a child with a disability a reasonable time before the public agency–

(i) Proposes to initiate or change the identification, evaluation, or educational placement of the child or the provision of FAPE to the child; or

(ii) Refuses to initiate or change the identification, evaluation, or educational placement of the child or the provision of FAPE to the child.

(2) If the notice described under paragraph (a) (1) of this section relates to an action proposed by the public agency that also requires parental consent under Section 300.505, the agency may give notice at the same time it requires parent consent.

(b) Content of notice. The notice required under paragraph (a) of this section must include–

(1) A description of the action proposed or refused by the agency;

(2) An explanation of why the agency proposes or refuses to take the action;

(3) A description of any other options that the agency considered and the reasons why those options were rejected;

(4) A description of each evaluation procedure, test, record, or report the agency used as a basis for the proposed or refused action;

(5) A description of any other factors that are relevant to the agency's proposal or refusal;

(6) A statement that the parents of a child with a disability have protection under the procedural safeguards of this part and, if this notice is not an initial referral for evaluation, the

means by which a copy of a description of the procedural safeguards can be obtained; and

(7) Sources for parents to contact to obtain assistance in understanding the provisions of this part.

(c) Notice in understandable language. (1) The notice required under paragraph (a) of this section must be—

(i) Written in language understandable to the general public; and

(ii) Provided in the native language of the parent or other mode of communication used by the parent, unless it is clearly not feasible to do so.

Complying with Section 504 and ADA

Office of Civil Rights Memorandum

From: Jeanette J. Lim, Acting Assistant Secretary for Civil Rights

Subject: Clarification of Responsibilities Concerning ADD Children

Date: April 29, 1993 (19.1DELR 876)

It recently has come to our attention that many school districts and parents appear to be misinterpreting a statement contained in the September 16, 1991, memorandum concerning "Clarification of Policy to Address the Needs of Children with Attention Deficit Disorders within General and/or Special Education." This statement, on page 6 of the memorandum, concerns the responsibility of local education agencies (LEAs) to evaluate children suspected of having ADD. The statement reads as follows:

Under Section 504, if parents believe that their child is disabled by ADD, the LEA must evaluate the child to determine whether he or she has a disability as defined by Section 504.

A similar version of this statement is contained in the Questions and Answers Handout [attachment] on ADD, entitled

"OCR Facts: Section 504 Coverage of Children with ADD." The Handout was attached to a model technical assistance (TA) presentation on ADD, disseminated to Regions on October 31, 1991, and is used as a TA resource.

The intent of this statement was to reaffirm that children suspected of having ADD and believed (by the LEA) to need special education or related services would have to be evaluated by the LEA pursuant to Section 504. These children are afforded protection and rights as any other children with disabilities under Section 504. This statement was necessary since many school districts, prior to issuance of the September 21, 1991, memorandum, held the position that they were not obliged to evaluate any child suspected of having ADD since it was not a disability specifically listed in the Individuals with Disabilities Education Act.

To our dismay, this statement has been interpreted to mean that school districts are required to evaluate every child suspected of having ADD, based solely on parental suspicion and demand. This was not the intent of the statement. Rather, under Section 504, if parents believe their child has a disability, whether by ADD or any other impairment, and the LEA has reason to believe the child needs special education or related services, the LEA must evaluate the child to determine whether he or she is disabled as defined by Section 504. If the LEA does not believe that the child needs special education or related services, and thus refuses to evaluate the child, the LEA must notify the parents of their due process rights.

This memorandum is intended to clarify the responsibility of LEAs to evaluate children suspected of having ADD, based on parental request. We have also taken the opportunity to revise the Handout, as appropriate. (See answer to the question "Must children thought to have ADD be evaluated by school districts?" on the first page of the Handout.) In addition, the Handout has been revised to reflect the term "disability" instead of "handicap," consistent with the 1992 Amendments to the Rehabilitation Act of 1973 (October 29, 1992). Please have your staff discard the October 1991 version of the Handout and replace it with the attached. If you have any questions regarding this memorandum, please contact Jean Peelen, Director, Elementary and Secondary Education Policy Division, at (202)-205-8637.

Attachment: OCR Facts:

Section 504 Coverage of Children with ADD

QUESTION: What is ADD?

ANSWER: Attention Deficit Disorder (ADD) is a term used to describe a chronic behavioral disorder in children who are inattentive, easily distracted, and impulsive. This kind of behavior is usually matched with certain other criteria, such as hyperactivity, before a child is diagnosed as having ADD. Symptoms of ADD may be manifested differently, depending on the particular subtype of the disorder and its severity. For example, with Attention Deficit Hyperactive Disorder (ADHD), hyperactivity is the primary characteristic. In this fact sheet, the term ADD is being used to refer to any form of the disorder.

QUESTION: Are all children with ADD automatically protected under Section 504?

ANSWER: NO. Some children with ADD may have a disability within the meaning of Section 504; others may not. Children must meet the Section 504 definition of disability to be protected under the regulation. Under Section 504, a "person with disabilities" is defined as any person who has a physical or mental impairment which substantially limits a major life activity (e.g., learning). Thus, depending on the severity of their condition, children with ADD may or may not fit within that definition.

QUESTION: Must children thought to have ADD be evaluated by school districts?

ANSWER: YES. If parents believe that their child has a disability, whether by ADD or any other impairment; and the school district has reason to believe that the child may need special education or related services, the school district must evaluate the child. If the school district does not believe the child needs special education or related services, and thus does not evaluate the child, the school district must notify the parents of their due process rights.

QUESTION: Must school districts have a different evaluation process for Section 504 and the IDEA?
ANSWER: NO. School districts may use the same process for evaluating the needs of students under Section 504 that they use for implementing IDEA.

QUESTION: Can school districts have a different evaluation process for Section 504?
ANSWER: YES. School districts may have a separate process for evaluating the needs of students under Section 504. However, they must follow the requirements for evaluation specified in the Section 504 regulation.

QUESTION: Is a child with ADD, who has a disability within the meaning of Section 504 but not under the IDEA, entitled to receive special education services?
ANSWER: YES. If a child with ADD is found to have a disability within the meaning of Section 504, he or she is entitled to receive any special education services the placement team decides are necessary.

QUESTION: Can a school district refuse to provide special education services to a child with ADD because he or she does not meet the eligibility criteria under the IDEA?
ANSWER: NO.

QUESTION: Can a child with ADD, who is protected under Section 504, receive related aids and services in the regular educational setting?
ANSWER: YES. Should it be determined that a child with ADD has a disability within the meaning of Section 504 and needs only adjustments in the regular classroom, rather than special education, those adjustments are required by Section 504.

QUESTION: Can parents request a due process hearing if a school district refuses to evaluate their child for ADD?
ANSWER: YES. In fact, parents may request a due process hearing to challenge any actions regarding the identification, evalu-

ation, or educational placement of their child with a disability, whom they believe needs special education or related services.

QUESTION: Must a school district have a separate hearing procedure for Section 504 and the IDEA?
ANSWER: NO. School districts may use the same procedures for resolving disputes under both Section 504 and the IDEA. In fact, many local school districts and some state education agencies are conserving time and resources by using the same due process procedures. However, education agencies should ensure that hearing officers are knowledgeable about the requirements of Section 504.

QUESTION: Can school districts use separate due process procedures for Section 504?
ANSWER: YES. School districts may have a separate system of procedural safeguards in place to resolve Section 504 disputes. However, these procedures must follow the requirements of the Section 504 regulation.

QUESTION: What should parents do if the state hearing process does not include Section 504?
ANSWER: Under Section 504, school districts are required to provide procedural safeguards and inform parents of these procedures. Thus, school districts are responsible for providing a Section 504 hearing even if the State process does not include it.

Appendix D

Resources

Suggested Reading

For more information about Attention Deficit/Hyperactivity Disorder and other related conditions, you may wish to consider the following:

Mary Fowler, *Maybe You Know My Kid*, Birchlane Press, Carol Publishing, 1993.

Barbara D. Ingersoll and Sam Goldstein (Contributor), *Lonely, Sad, and Angry*, Main Street Books, 1996.

For more information about parenting, I find the following books to be invaluable:

Deepak Chopra, *The Seven Spiritual Laws for Parents*, Harmony Books, 1997.

Harville Hendrix, Ph.D, and Helen Hunt, M.A., M.L.A., *Giving the Love that Heals*, Pocket Books, 1997.

Linda Kavelin Popov, *The Family Virtues Guide*, Penguin Books, 1997.

Support Groups

Children and Adults with Attention Deficit Disorder
  (CHADD)
8181 Professional Pl., Suite 201
Landover, MD 20785
Phone: 800-233-4050
Website: www.chadd.org

The National Attention Deficit Disorder Association (ADDA)
PO Box 972
Mentor, OH 44061
Phone: 440-350-9595
Website: www.add.org

Learning Disabilities Association
4156 Library Road
Pittsburgh, PA 15234
Phone: 412-341-1515
Website: www.ldanatl.org

About the Author

Tammy Young is the mother of two children with Attention Deficit/Hyperactivity Disorder. She has worked extensively with the issues inherent to this disorder for the past eight years as a parent, a special education teacher, an educational consultant, and an advocate. She provides counseling and consultations for parents as well as seminars for educators. Tammy lives with her three children in Austin, Texas, and loves to hear from her readers. You can send e-mail to tammy@livingwithadhd.com and visit her at her website www.livingwithadhd.com.